The Opening Night Murders

by

James Scott Byrnside

COVER ART AND DESIGN BY

MATT WILLIS-JONES

INFO@MATTWILLISJONES.COM

SPECIAL THANKS TO

JAIMIE-LEE WISE

DEDICATED TO

MARY BER

This book is a work of fiction. The characters, incidents, and dialogue are not to be construed as real. Any resemblance to people living or dead is entirely coincidental. All rights reserved. No part of this book may be used or reproduced in any manner whatsoever without written permission except in the case of brief quotations embodied in critical articles or reviews.

TABLE OF CONTENTS

Playbill	The Balcony	1
Chapter 1	Actress	3
Chapter 2	Final Rehearsal	27
Chapter 3	Just a Coincidence	43
Chapter 4	Opening Night	61
Chapter 5	What Happened?	79
Chapter 6	Six or Zero	103
Chapter 7	The Director	123
Chapter 8	David Brouthers's Shindig	143
Chapter 9	What You Don't Know Gets You Killed	157
Chapter 10	It's Blunt, Not Obvious	171
Chapter 11	The Nasty, Dark-Haired Girl	189
Chapter 12	Re-cast	199
Chapter 13	Eyewitness	209
Chapter 14	Doctor Brown	219
Chapter 15	And Then There Were Two	229
Chapter 16	Curtain	235
Chapter 17	End of Inquiry	261

NOTE TO THE READER

FOR YOUR CONVENIENCE, A PLAYBILL OF *THE BALCONY* HAS BEEN PROVIDED. THE CAST AND CREW ARE MAJOR PLAYERS IN THIS NOVEL.

JAMES SCOTT BYRNSIDE

THE PLAYBILL

A SMASHING ENTERTAINMENT
...JUST WHAT WE NEED IN
THESE TROUBLED TIMES
- CHARLES GUTWORTH
CHICAGO TRIBUNE

DESTINED TO BE THE MOST
ROMANTIC AND UPLIFTING
PLAY OF 1935
- BRENDA O'LEARY
DAILY HERALD

ROMANCE, LAUGHTER,
HEARTBREAK...THE BALCONY IS
A REMINDER OF WHY WE GO TO
THE THEATER
- MARTIN BREGMAN
THE NEW SUN

THE RED RISING THEATRE COMPANY PROUDLY PRESENTS

THE BALCONY

WRITTEN AND DIRECTED BY JENNY PLUVIAM

CAST

LISA PLUVIAM	as	MARGARET HUNT
TIMOTHY BROWN	as	CLARK HUNT
EDWARD FILIUS	as	CAREY JOHNSON
ALLISON MILLER	as	STELLA JOHNSON
MAURA LEWIS	as	LANA HUNT

CREW

PRODUCED	by	JENNY PLUVIAM and LISA PLUVIAM
LIGHTING AND SET DESIGN	by	SAM "GRIZZ" THOMPSON
WRITTEN	by	JENNY PLUVIAM
DIRECTED	by	JENNY PLUVIAM

1

ACTRESS

5:01 p.m. Wednesday, April 3rd, 1935

Detective Rowan Manory pinched some tobacco between gnarled, nicotine-stained fingers and held it above a cigarette paper. He tried to keep his hand steady, but the more he tried, the more it shook. The tobacco dropped, sprinkling off the side of the paper onto his desk. *Damnit.*

As he slid the dried leaves into a small mound with his pinkies, an all-too-familiar dread hovered like a noose in the back of his mind. *Do not think about it, old man. It is simply a mechanism.* In a swift, persistent motion, Rowan dropped the tobacco across the paper, rolled it, and licked the glue strip. He stared at the completed cigarette, more concerned than satisfied.

Life is turning into a bad joke. I fear I am the disappointing punch line. Soon I will not even be able to roll my own cigarettes. I'll be forced to smoke pre-rolled. They taste of hot dust.

The afternoon edition of *The Chicago Tribune* lay unfolded on Rowan's desk. As usual, he could find nothing positive printed within its pages. The city remained the murder capital of the United States, a true feat in these violent, troubled times. The bombing of the Federal Building downtown dominated the front page. It had happened that very morning, so details remained sketchy. Although no one claimed credit, hints of unsubstantiated terrorism floated through the article.

Perhaps my advancing age is a good thing. The average man lives to be fifty-eight. Rowan did the math. *I have eleven summers left. God only knows what the city will look like then. And what of me? What other wonderful ailments are in store for me?*

Two shadows moved behind the door's stained glass. Soft murmurs of unintelligible conversation drifted into Rowan's office. Without knocking, Walter Williams cracked opened the door to slip his gangly body into the room. "There's a woman here to see you, old man." He whispered and his eyes glinted with suggestion. "Says she knows you."

"What is her name?"

Walter waggled his brows and lowered his voice even more. "She's an attractive specimen."

"The name?"

"Age appropriate, as well."

"Williams—"

"Lisa Pluviam."

Rowan straightened his aching back against the chair. Why was she here? More importantly, how did he look? A plan of action was needed and quickly. "Stall her for two minutes."

Walter grinned. "Right."

A desk mirror, pulled from the middle drawer, revealed a blotchy, frowning face. Several wiry hairs stuck out defiantly from his nostrils, and his eyes leaned back into cavernous sockets. The harsh, revealing sunlight from the window wasn't helping, so he shut the blinds and began a frantic search for his trusty mustache scissors. He yanked each desk drawer open in vain. *Shit.* Rowan put his fingers in his nose and ripped out hairs in tiny bunches, causing him to sneeze uncontrollably. *Another consequence of age. One stops caring for oneself after a while. You accept the image in the mirror every morning. When was the last time—* His jowls constricted in horror. *Do I smell old? Do I reek of that unbearable mixture of orris root, cucumber, and fat, simmered to a disgusting room temperature?* He splashed a bit of Pour un Homme over his throat, assaulting his olfactory nerves with a burning stench of lavender.

Walter's well-timed knock came at the door. The detective dropped into his seat, wiped his face with a handkerchief, and swept the mirror back into the drawer with a loud clang of brass and a tiny crack of glass. With the newspaper neatly folded into a rectangle at the corner of his desk, Rowan sucked in his considerable gut. "Come in."

Lisa Pluviam's hair appeared black but came with the scent of ammonia, a dead giveaway that it was graying and she was now forced to dye it. The smell was not overbearing, as it was tempered by Femme Du Jour. This created a new odor which, though not quite intoxicating, smelled vaguely floral. She had a dark face with a mouth made sunken by pronounced cheek-bones. The blue of her irises contained within them flaws of green and brown, giving her an almost otherworldly sense of gravity and importance. Rowan thought her gorgeous.

"It's good to see you, Rowan," she said, resting her scarlet-taloned hands on the arms of the chair. "I'm sorry it took me such a long time to pay you a visit."

"Not as sorry as I am, madam." He turned to Walter with a satisfied smirk. "Williams, sitting across from me is the finest actress in all of Chicago."

Lisa blew a raspberry. "My God. That's not hard to live up to at all."

Rowan pointed his index finger upward. "And yet, I speak the truth. So smitten was I with your performance in *The Farmer's Daughter*, I coerced my way backstage in order to make your acquaintance."

Walter concurred. "Manory can't stand people. If he went out of his way to meet you, it must have been an impressive show."

Lisa glanced around the office, taking in her surroundings. A large, blank-faced clock ticked away next to two photos of smartly-dressed women, pinned rather lazily to the wall. Two half-full bottles of Dreighton sat atop the overstuffed cabinet near the window. The colors of the room were dulled, as if a layer of dust had adhered to every surface. She pointed one of those bright red nails at the photographs. "Old girlfriends?"

Rowan shook his head, a dumb smile plastered to his face. "An old case."

"Were they satisfied with your work?" Lisa asked.

"They were murdered."

"Excuse me?"

"I revisit completed assignments from time to time to determine if any errors in judgment were made. This has been an abnormally slow week, so I have had time to reminisce. These women were casualties of a particularly disturbed mind. Perhaps you've heard of the Barrington Hills Vampire?"

Something between awe and disbelief flashed over her face. "You and I must get together for a drink sometime. You can tell me all your detective stories. Some very desperate people must have sat in this chair, asking for your help."

"Nothing would make me happier. Perhaps, we could make an appointment after one of your performances. I plan to attend your newest play."

Walter took out the notebook he always kept at the ready. He scribbled a quick note and showed it to Rowan. *For God's sake, don't call it an appointment.*

Lisa said, "Yes, the play. That's why I'm here. I was hoping you would agree to come to the opening performance on Friday."

A masculine confidence rolled through Rowan's body. He pushed his shoulders out wide and puffed his chest like a cat wanting to appear bigger. "It is a date, Miss Pluviam."

She rolled her eyes. "Don't call me Miss Pluviam. I'm not a school teacher."

"Duly noted, Lisa. Williams and I would be thrilled to attend. Wouldn't we, Williams?"

Walter winced. "I'm more of a moving-picture man myself. Don't get me wrong, I admire the theater. I just have a terrible time staying awake."

A bit of graveness crept into Lisa's cheery demeanor, her flawed eyes drifting from Rowan to a speck on the mahogany floor. "I'm not here strictly for a social visit. In fact, now I am one of those desperate people sitting in this chair, asking for your help." She pulled out a gray slip of paper from her purse. In the process of unfolding it, she stopped, her hands forming into soft fists and crumpling it between thin, attractive fingers.

Intrigued, Rowan tilted his head at the mysterious note in her hand. "Anything you say here will be held in the strictest confidence." His voice conveyed pillowed reassurance. "I am more than happy to offer my advice or assistance. Would you care for a drink? Coffee? Tea?"

"No, thank you. I—"

"Milk? Whiskey?"

"I don't know quite what to make of this, but it has me a little spooked." Lisa gave a joyless, perfunctory smile. "It's probably nothing, a waste of your time."

Rowan extended his hand toward the paper and curled stubby fingers into a come-hither motion. "Let me see." She reached over, laying it open on the desk. He stared at the paper, speechless. The one hand remained in midair with extended fingers while the other twiddled the butt of his cigarette until it formed a little stem. He was not much edified by what he read.

LiSa PlUVIuM

oN OpEnING night

YOU WiLl DIE

Walter came round and read the cut-out newspaper letters over his boss's shoulder. Rowan lit the cigarette and puffed at the wispy, bent end. "Most troubling."

Lisa said, "I've been trying to come up with theories. I don't owe anyone money. As far as I know I'm not part of the underworld or anything crazy. I was thinking…I suppose I was *hoping* it could be a joke, someone just having a go at me for fun."

Rowan's mind was taken back to that nasty Lasciva business from 1927. "Possibly, but that is not the premise upon which you should be basing your actions."

It took her a moment to respond. People often took time to decipher Rowan's speech. "You think I should be worried?"

"I do," Rowan replied. "What's more, I think you should cancel the play and report this to the police post haste. They would be far more capable of assisting you in this matter."

Her gaze switched from Rowan back to the tiny speck. "That would be the intelligent thing to do, I'm sure. Unfortunately, I can't."

Walter and Rowan looked at her with the same humorless expression and both had the same troubling thought. *A person who cannot go to the police is a person who cannot be trusted.*

Lisa explained. "I'm not going to cancel the show over an anonymous threat. And I know damn well the police aren't going to come and provide security. They'll demand the show be stopped. If it were only me, that wouldn't be a problem. However, there are the other actors to consider—not to mention my sister. It's Jenny's directorial debut. She'd be devastated."

"Lisa—"

She leaned forward, placing her hands flat on his desk. "If you came Friday night and kept an eye on me, sort of like a bodyguard."

"It is not exactly our specialty. We investigate crimes after the fact. We do not prevent them." Rowan's eyes shifted back to the note. "Do you have any guess as to the identity of the author?"

"I wish I did. The whole thing is baffling. If someone wanted me dead, I'm sure I'd have heard about it long before now."

"Then let us narrow things down a bit and see what we can determine. Where and when did you find this message?"

"This afternoon. It was on my desk, lying on top of my script."

"And where is your desk located?"

"In my office. At the back of the auditorium, there are two offices adjacent to one another. My sister's is on the left, and mine is on the right. After we finished rehearsal, I went into my office, just like I do every day. Only today, this wonderful note was waiting for me."

Rowan pictured the layout in his head. "When was the last time you had been in your office before this afternoon?"

"Yesterday. About three o'clock."

He stubbed out his cigarette and rolled another with no hint of the previous tremors. "Brilliant. We know the note was left sometime between yesterday afternoon and today, roughly a twenty-four hour period. Williams, what is the next logical query?"

Walter pulled his notebook out again. "Who had access to the theater during the established time frame?"

"Everyone who was there yesterday has keys." Lisa counted them on her fingers. "That's six people in total, seven if you include me."

"Does anyone work at the theater after rehearsal, alone at night, when they would have more freedom to act?" Rowan asked.

"I suppose Grizz spends the most time there."

"Grizz?"

"He's the head of technical production. He's in charge of the sets, the props, the lighting."

"Yes, but...*Grizz*?"

"I guess it's a funny nickname, isn't it?" Lisa chuckled. "His real name is Sam, but everyone calls him Grizz."

Walter said, "Why?"

"I've never asked. I guess it's 'cause he's grizzled, you know? He's got one of those leathery faces, a lot of cracks in it that you can read. A million lines, a million stories. That sort of thing."

Rowan lit the new cigarette. The sublime satisfaction of smoke flooded into his blackened lungs. "What of the other members of production? Grips, front of house, those kinds of people?"

Lisa waved at the cloud in front of her face. "We'll have two grips and a box office manager for opening night, but the main crew finished last week. I think Grizzy had a team of about six or seven people."

"One of them may have come at night when the theater is empty," Rowan suggested.

"None of them have keys. Jenny and I gave keys to the actors and the technician. No one else."

"I see." Rowan pondered this thought as drops of rain pinged against the windows, the sounds amplified by the stillness in the room.

Lisa bit her bottom lip. "What are you thinking, detective?"

"I am considering the psychology of this particular death threat. It is quite odd. Typically, threats such as these involve finances. They include demands for money. Sometimes, there is a political message attached. The threat is made for the purpose of bringing light to some ideological cause."

"Neither is true in my case."

"Correct." Rowan stood, circling Lisa's chair in measured shuffle steps. She turned her neck to follow him. "Yours is only being used to inform you of your impending death. Naturally, there is a question of practicality. What could possibly be gained by revealing to you the day of your murder?"

"Don't know. If I wanted to kill someone, I wouldn't advertise it."

Rowan returned to his chair, stubbing out his barely-smoked cigarette. "Precisely. The *only* thing to gain is your fear. The author of this note requires you to suffer."

Lisa shifted uncomfortably in her seat. "What did I ever do to deserve this attention, assuming it's genuine?"

"That should be our advantage. The motive must be intensely personal, enough to cause a pathological hatred. Surely, it would be retaliation for some act you have committed or been perceived to have committed, something you would undoubtedly be aware of." When Lisa did not come forward with a suggestion, Rowan gently prodded her. "An unrequited love or some other act of betrayal?"

She shook her head with confidence. "I don't have those kinds of skeletons in my closet."

"Uh-huh." Rowan flicked his tongue against his cheek and scratched his balding head. *Everyone has something in the past that will not stay quiet.* "Last year, you were working with the Saunter Stock Troupe. They produced *The Farmer's Daughter*?"

13

"That's right."

"Flip the calendar ahead one year. You and your sister have your own company and your own theatre space. It must have cost a pretty penny. If you do not mind my asking, how were you able to raise the capital for such an endeavor?"

Lisa held her gaze hard in concentration, did a double take, then giggled helplessly.

The underlying tension that had built up in the room let out. Rowan looked to Walter. "Did I say something amusing, Williams?"

She wiped her eyes and cleared her throat. "I'm sorry." Her laughing fit started again but she fought through it. "It's just the way you talk." Walter grinned as Lisa leaned forward, almost childlike, and deepened her voice to mimic Rowan's. *"How were you able to raise the capital for such an endeavor?* What a strange way to ask me how I got the money."

He turned a shade red. "I am verbose."

"You talk a lot, too. It's from my writing days. I can't stand two words when one will do just fine."

"Uh… How *did* you get the money?"

"It was from an inheritance. Our dad died last winter. To my surprise, he left everything to me. The Red Rising Theatre was born."

"My sympathies about your father." *Does she not see the obvious angle?*

"It was for the best. We didn't communicate with him a lot

during his last years, but, as I understand it, he was in a great deal of pain." Lisa spoke with sudden determination, as if trying to convince Rowan of her sincerity. "Jenny and I have been working in theater for a long time. We started in high school. Then we farted around flops and dives in Chicago for seven years. I did every job you could imagine. I sewed buttons, I took tickets. A few times I sat in the audience and laughed at the jokes. After a while, we went to New York and studied. Later we taught. Add in the little shows we put on for our parents when we were children, and you could say we've been in theater our entire lives. You can imagine how much this newfound freedom and independence meant to us. This is the first time we've been able to do exactly as we wish. Our father's money could not have been put to better use."

Rowan twisted a cigarette together and brought a bit of the tension back. "But..."

"But what?"

"From your wording, am I to deduce that your sister did not receive any part of the inheritance?"

She flinched, and beneath her airy confidence appeared a slight anxiety. "No, she didn't."

"Did that trouble her?" Rowan asked.

"Not a bit. In fact, it's rather a great source of entertainment for her."

"How is that?"

"As Jenny likes to remind me, our father left everything to the *older* daughter. But that's Jenny. She's always been a smart aleck."

Walter licked the tip of his pencil. "I'm sorry to interrupt, but could you put a bee in my bonnet and tell me the full names of everyone we're dealing with. The names are important. Your sister is Jenny Pluviam?"

"Yes, she's the writer and director."

Rowan said, "Do you live together?"

Lisa nodded. "We always have. Our father owned a house on the north side. We moved there when we returned to Chicago."

Walter said, "And this gentleman with the face?"

"I met Grizz on *The Farmer's Daughter*, and I was impressed with his work. His full name is Sam Thompson. We hired him as a carpenter to build the sets, but he ended up wearing many different hats."

"You recommended him to Jenny?" asked Rowan.

"Yes, I did. He's a talented man, a little cranky, but Grizz gets the job done."

"I take it from your description that he is older?"

"He's got to be in his early sixties."

Walter wrote *suspects* at the top of the page. "And the actors?"

"Maura Lewis plays my daughter. Maura's the only one not from Chicago. I think she moved here from Iowa or Ohio. I'm not sure."

A snickering breath escaped Walter's lips. "Not really much of a difference, is there? It's either corn fields or corn fields."

"She told me once, but I can't remember," Lisa said, without much apparent interest.

Rowan continued, "Is she a nice girl?"

Lisa nodded. "It takes a while to get to know her. Maura can come off a little abrasive at first, but deep down, she's sweet. Just needs a little guidance. Next, there's Edward Filius." She spelled the last name. "He plays my neighbor. We fall in love during the course of the play."

"Why is the play called *The Balcony*?"

"The gist is, Edward and I meet on the balconies of our apartments, and slowly get to know one another. On the right side of the stage, there's a twenty-foot-high tower with the two balconies side by side. It's quite the visual."

"Did you know Edward, previously?"

"No. The only people I knew were Jenny and Grizz. None of the actors were my choice. My sister is directing so she makes the decisions."

You provide the money, but Jenny is the boss. "Did you disapprove of the casting decisions?"

Lisa froze for a moment. "What does this have to do with the note I found?"

"Humor me, Lisa," Rowan said. "I am simply trying to gain a comprehensive understanding of the situation. If there is any animosity, however deeply buried, it could be the cause of this threat."

"I did disapprove, but I'm happy to say my initial feelings were wrong. I was particularly worried about working with

Edward, this being his first play. It didn't bother Jenny; she recognized his talent straight away. The only thing an actor needs is a set of ears. I mean metaphorical ears, of course. You can be deaf and act. Edward has big ears."

"Metaphorically speaking?"

"Yes. He's a natural. The other two actors are professionals. Timothy Brown and Allison Miller. They both graduated from the Goodman School. They've done two or three plays, small scale stuff. They're really good though. Everyone's really good. People are going to like this play. In fact—"

Rowan lifted an eyebrow. "Sweethearts?"

"Sweethearts?" She blinked.

"Are Allison and Timothy sweethearts?"

"Yes, how did you know?"

"You said their names together."

Lisa smiled. "Of course, I did. I hadn't noticed. Yes, they've been a couple for a long time."

"But not married."

"No."

Rowan sensed a hollow and dug a bit. "How have things been between them during production?"

"What do you mean?"

She knows exactly what I mean. Why would she bide for time? "They say that couples should never work together. You know how they bicker now and then."

"If there are any problems, they don't bring them to work."

Rowan pretended to pick at a cuticle with his thumbnail. "A pity they don't play a couple on the stage."

Lisa furrowed her brow. "I didn't say that, did I?"

"And yet it is true. Maura plays your daughter and Edward plays your neighbor. That leaves you short one husband and Edward, one wife. Naturally, Timothy plays your husband, and Allison plays Edward's wife."

"That's right." She eyed him with curiosity. "You're quick."

"Not as quick as I once was." *If only we had met twenty years ago.* "Describe them for me. Paint me a picture of Allison and Timothy."

"Allison is a bit flighty. Everything that happens to her becomes dramatized, and then *endlessly* discussed."

"Typical actor behavior then?"

Lisa tapped her nose and gave a knowing, lopsided grin.

Rowan copied her grin without thinking. *It is as if I am a puppet that will perform as suggested.* Having started this train of thought, he couldn't stop. *Does she realize she has this power over me, or is it natural to her like a siren singing sailors to their deaths? Have I been doing it this whole time? Good lord. And why—*

"Don't you think?" Lisa asked.

"What?"

Lisa repeated herself.

Rowan stammered. "I… Yes. Of course. That is always true, is it not?"

Her nose wrinkled in confusion. "It's always true that Allison should be more confident on stage?"

He fumbled with a pencil on his desk, catching up to where they were in the conversation. "No, but women in general need to be more confident."

"*I* don't need to be more confident. My confidence is perfect." Lisa gave a subtle tug at her flutter skirt, exposing a bit more of her thigh.

Walter rescued Rowan. "And Timothy Brown?"

"Timothy… God, how do I describe Tim—? He grew up on a farm and in his heart, he's still out working the fields, getting his hands dirty. I can't say he's terribly bright, but he doesn't need to be. He's what the kids nowadays would call *cheesecake*. That's everybody." She threw her arms in the air and let them fall to her side. "None of them have a reason to want me dead."

"You said this death threat was lying on your script. Tell me, was the script opened?" asked Rowan.

"It sure was."

"To which scene was it opened?"

"The first balcony scene. Act one, scene four."

"Think back. Was the script opened to that scene when you left the office yesterday afternoon?"

She looked into the air as if trying to remember the image. "I don't think so. No. In fact, I'm sure it was closed yesterday." She gasped. "Whoever left the note must have opened the script to that page. Is that important?"

"We shall see."

She nodded, lost in thought and then shifted her cracked eyes directly at his. "Rowan?"

"Yes?"

"Have you deduced anything about me?"

He paused. *Yes. There is something or other you are afraid of saying. I have a vague impression you said it once accidently, and I should have observed it then, but I let it go.* "What would I possibly deduce about you?"

"I'm an actress; I'm curious about what I communicate."

Rowan's voice trailed off. "Just a few frivolous things. Nothing important."

Lisa's interest piqued. "Tell me."

"All right. You play a rich woman in *The Balcony*."

"What's your evidence?"

"When we met last summer, I noticed that your ears were not pierced. The slight scarring on your lobes suggests that you have recently had them pierced just for this play, and your body is rejecting the change. I imagine this was done to demonstrate wealth."

Lisa covered her ears. Her mouth gaped. "I never wear jewelry. My skin doesn't react well. When I wear the earrings it covers up the scarring. I should be more mindful when I'm not wearing them."

"Use hydrogen peroxide to kill the infection. Iodine is murder on the epidermis. I can also tell you wear a necklace." Rowan pointed at her chest. "There is a nearly imperceptible greenish hue. The necklace must be at least partially made of copper alloy. Copper is easily made to look like gold on stage. When it comes into contact with perspiration, oxidation occurs and it sometimes stains the skin. You have done your utmost to hide it with powder, but—"

"But when someone stares at your tits long enough, he'll notice it?"

"No. No…I…"

"Relax, dollface. I'm just joshing you. Anything else?" Lisa smiled with a Cheshire grin.

Rowan sat back in his chair, scarlet with mortification. "I can tell that you are not terribly worried about this note. That will change. As opening night gets closer, you will begin to dwell on the horrific implications of this threat. What is now theoretical will soon become reality."

"I *do* take it seriously. I was hoping you would tell me not to worry."

"Someone has threatened your life, and this someone must have had access to the theater in the allotted time frame. That means six suspects. Grizz has perhaps the strongest opportunity, given he works in the theater alone during the evening. Motive is unknown."

"Grizz and I are good friends."

"Your sister Jenny."

"Jenny wouldn't—"

Rowan raised his hand, cutting her off in mid-sentence. "For the moment, let us leave out our wouldn'ts and couldn'ts and just speak in mights. Motive is very strong. Opportunity ditto."

"She's family."

Walter said, "Money is thicker than blood."

Rowan nodded. "My awkwardly-tongued friend is correct. Trust me, the motive is strong. As to the others, Edward will be the closest to you during the balcony scene. Based on your description, you will be twenty feet in the air and quite vulnerable to an attack." He picked up the pencil and dropped it on the table. "One push is all it would take."

"He can't push me. There's a partition between us that divides our balconies."

"Nevertheless, this is the very scene on which the threat was so lovingly placed. It could be a message within the message. I imagine the others will also have ample opportunity, if not on the stage, then in the seclusion offered by the curtain. What are the ages of the actors?"

"They're all in their early twenties." Lisa snorted. "So there I am, a fifty-two year old woman farting around on stage with a bunch of kids."

Rowan twirled the pencil back and forth with his thumbs. "Why did you come to me?"

"Because I trust you."

"You barely know me; we have only met once."

"You make a good impression. I can tell you know what

you're doing, that you are reliable. I don't think anything is going to happen on opening night, but on the off-chance someone *does* want to kill me, I'd feel a whole lot better if you were there watching over me."

Rowan drummed his fingers on the desk.

Lisa smiled. "So?"

He smiled back. "We will take your case."

"Wonderful."

"There are conditions."

"Shoot."

"The cast must be addressed as to the situation," Rowan said. "If one of them has planned a murder, I want him to know that *I know*. I will inform them on Friday afternoon. That way no alternate plans will be made. Williams will be backstage during the play. When you are not onstage, he will be your shadow."

"And where will you be?" Lisa asked.

"I'll be watching from the front row. Nothing is going to happen to you. Now," he pulled a card from his wallet, "please write down your address. Walter will come round at seven o'clock to pick up a copy of the script which he will read tonight."

Walter's eyes shot over to Rowan. "I will?"

"That is correct. Tomorrow, after rehearsal, we shall have a look around the theater. Say, one o'clock?"

Lisa jotted down her address. "Terrific. That's just terrific. We haven't discussed your fee."

The detective shook his head. "We will arrange something

later. Perhaps the drink you mentioned previously."

Lisa shook Walter's hand. "Tonight then." She turned to Rowan and bypassed his extended hand to plant a delicate kiss on his baggy cheek. "And I'll see you tomorrow."

Rowan fixated on the empty door frame as the click-clack of her heels faded down the steps. He turned to Walter's disbelieving stare. "What is the matter, Williams?"

Walter's emotions were eminently readable. The lines of his face had become more pronounced with age, but they could not hide the smooth hints of perfectly placed, cherubic baby fat that continued to project a boyishness even now in his early forties. When he was worried about something, everyone in the room knew. "Are you sure this is wise, Manory?"

"Perhaps not. There are some irregularities in Miss Pluviam's story."

"Irregularities? I'm dumber than a second coat of paint, and even I realize this is off-kilter."

"You know as well as I, people react differently to life threatening situations. She's an actress. They are emotional and...and...complex."

"I've never seen you take a case based on indulging in the client's charms. It's not your style."

"She *is* very charming, isn't she?"

"And you think she likes you?"

"I have no idea what the woman likes. I know she is possibly in danger, and she requires my assistance."

"She came to see you after one chance encounter—out of the proverbial blue."

"There is nothing about *the blue* in proverbs. There is nothing proverbial about the phrase."

Walter fell back into Rowan's chair, kicking his long legs up onto the desk. "God, you're a hard man to talk to, Manory."

"Words have meanings. Otherwise, why use them?"

"At least trim your nose hair. It's really unbecoming."

Rowan's face turned hard. "Williams, where are my mustache scissors?"

Walter's eyes drifted to the door in the pale, slowly waning process of remembrance. "I think they might be in the kitchenette."

"The kitchenette?"

"Yes, I'm quite sure that's where I left them."

"Why would the mustache scissors be in the kitchenette? What possible purpose could they serve there?"

"I use them to open the coffee, old man. They fit the slot of the canister perfectly. You used to drink Gerbolds, and I could use a butter knife to open those containers. After they went out of business, you switched brands to Silver Cup. The lid is all funny; knives don't work because the slot is too thin. Your mustache scissors are the perfect size. You can see my dilemma."

Rowan glared at Walter.

"What?"

"Were you born this way, Williams, or is this the culmination of all your hard work?"

2

FINAL REHEARSAL

7:35 a.m. Thursday, April 4th

Edward Filius took hold of his Aunt Christine's hand, her skin squishing onto the bone like glop under his fingers. He gently raised it in the direction of the marquee above the door. "I told you I would do it, Christine."

The old woman doddered her head back. "*The Balcony*. Written and directed by Jenny Pluviam. Starring Lisa Pluviam." Her mouth tightened into mild disapproval. "Why aren't you on the marquee, dear?" Christine forgot why they were at the theater as soon as she asked the question. It was far too early for her to be out and about, away from the snug, cool sheets of her bed. Her feeble muscles tightened in frustration as she looked up and down Halsted. The line for free breakfast stretched from the butcher's window past the end of the block. A woman stood near the curb with her young daughter. They balanced a handmade cardboard sign in front of them. *MUST WE STARVE?* Christine circled round until she came back to the pale young man smiling at her. "What did you ask me?"

Edward spoke to his aunt with a well-rehearsed but genuinely felt patience. "We were discussing the marquee. It isn't big enough, and there's only room for two names. That's why I'm not up there. If the company were bigger, they'd probably list all the actors."

Christine's eyes showed a bit of life as cognitive wrinkles formed round her temples. She remembered again. Edward was her nephew, but more like her son, and he was starring in a play. Or was he? "But you are in the play, dear?"

"Yes. For sure, Christine. I've got a big part."

Maternal confidence returned to her voice. "Oh, I'm so proud of you. Your mother would be proud too. I just know it. I'm terribly excited to see the inside. It's been ages since I was in a theater."

Past the front of house, a short hallway led to two-hundred seats facing a fifty-foot stage. The auditorium was a grand hall with a burnished, golden-brown hardwood floor. A single wide light shined over the three clearly defined sets. At stage left, a dining table covered with silverware and plates, in the center, a living room with a posh-looking sofa, and on the right, a twenty-foot black tower with the titular balcony on top. Two offices overlooked the audience from the back, and far above the seats, a horseshoe-shaped catwalk housed the lights. The ends of the catwalk hung ten feet from the stage.

Christine strained into the last seat of the darkened back row. "This was a splendid idea. If I came during a real performance," she tittered, "it would be too much for my nerves. I hope I don't fall asleep. You know how awful I snore."

"Does it bring back memories?" asked Edward.

"Memories of what, dear? I've never been here, have I?"

He sighed. "I meant memories of your acting days."

A chortle escaped her mouth. "I was never a real actor. Not like you. Not like…this. Although, I will say that balcony reminds me of a play I did at The Renaud. It was called *Jezebel* something or other. I was a princess in a tower. There were knights all around me, riding on broomsticks, no less. It took quite a bit of concentration not to burst out laughing at them all clicking around the stage."

He tried to check his watch in the dark. "I suppose it's time for me to get ready. Will you be all right back here alone?"

Christine thought long and hard about the question. "Where's the toilet?" Edward motioned toward a door near the fire exit. "Then I'll be fine. Don't fret over me." Her knuckles trembled against her lips. "I had some advice for you. What was it?"

"You can tell me later. I really should get to the dressing

room. Costume, make-up, the whole shebang."

"No, I've got it." Her eyes lit up. "I've remembered now. If you forget a line, say something in the spirit of what the line was. The audience doesn't care when you flub bits of dialogue. They only care about the sweep of the thing. Good luck, dear."

Edward headed down the aisle, hopping onto the pine floor of the stage. As he wiped a bit of psychosomatic sweat from his head, the sound of Maura Lewis's fluty, liquid voice came from behind a slit in the curtain.

"What's doing, Eddie?" Maura absently chewed the ends of her blue-black bob. The torn nylon over her knee, which had been yanked repeatedly, revealed a small rainbow-colored bruise. She leaned to one side, pulling on the curtain to maintain her tortured posture. "Did you bring your auntie?"

Edward waved an arm at the seats. "She's in the back. Not feeling very sociable, I'm afraid."

Maura called out. "Hello, Miss Filius!" Her voice reverberated before vanishing into the darkness of the auditorium. After a few seconds she asked, "Why isn't she answering me?"

"Dunno. She might already be asleep."

"You said she was old, but is she uh…" Maura twirled a finger around the temple of her lovely head. "Plum loco en la cabeza? I mean, official like?"

Edward moved closer, whispering so Christine wouldn't hear. "Just a rough day. She's fine."

"Eddie, I wanted to ask you something," Her eyes drifted

downward over her freckled face. "Are you still going to the hospital after rehearsal."

"Yeah."

"For a delivery?"

He nodded. "Garfield Hospital. Why?"

"Acksherly, I was planning on going that way, and I was wondering if I could get a ride."

"Of course, I—"

"But then I was thinking that maybe you wanted to go with me." Maura's foot kicked an invisible object. "See, David Brouthers is having himself a shindig tonight." She made eye contact. "Do you want to come?"

Edward's mouth moved, but he didn't say anything. The plan had been to ask Maura out after the play was finished. He had never expected her to take the first step.

The silence lasted so long that she finally blurted out, "You don't have to, I'm just spitballing."

"I thought the party was next week."

A wry smile formed at one corner of her mouth. "Well, yeah, a fella, he can have more than one party. David's having one next week and he's having one tonight. I just thought I'd ask you—"

"What kind of crowd is it?"

"Oh, you've never seen anything like a David Brouthers shindig. Guaranteed. His dad owns a building up north...Wait, why am I whispering?"

"Because I was whispering. You're copying me

subconsciously."

"I'm such a lamebrain. Anywho, the building is um… whatdyacallit?" She snapped her fingers. "Oh, you know."

"Apartments? Offices?"

"That's it—dilapidated. The plumbing doesn't work and the floor's ripped up. It's going to get torn down next year so David doesn't care what happens to the joint. His shindigs can get a lil' crazy. Acksherly, a lot crazy. After everyone gets drunk enough, there's usually a séance or—"

"Yes."

"Yes, what?"

"Yes, I'll go with you."

"Really?" Maura gave him a toothy grin. "Swell. I promise we'll have fun. I'll tag along with you and your auntie after rehearsal."

Edward frowned. "Oh, but I still have to stop at the hospital. Then I have to drop Christine off at home. What time do we have to be there?"

"We can show up any old time. And, I don't mind waiting. It's no skin off my ear."

He tilted his head at her. "Nose."

"Huh?"

"Nose. It's no skin off my nose."

"I'm pretty sure it's *ear*," Maura said.

"Never. No one has ever said that before you said it just now."

"Why would skin come off your nose?"

"Why would it come off your ear?"

She shrugged. "Maybe it's an Ohio saying."

They squeezed through the narrow wing on the way to the dressing room where Allison Miller sat next to her beau, fiddling with a rhinestone hair clip in front of her mirror. A large assortment of old clothing filled the wardrobe, causing a must to linger over the redolent sawdust trapped in the nooks and crannies throughout the room.

Maura wrapped her arms around Allison from behind, pecking her on the cheek. "Adorable."

"Oh, please." Allison's hair was so dense and stridently cut that it made a sort of wool-knit cap around the top of her head. Jenny had suggested the look as a representation of upper-class chic. "I miss my long locks. Look at me." She pouted. "I'm a little Roman boy come to life."

Timothy Brown's head remained buried in the morning paper. "I call her Claudius. Still ought to need a shield for the full effect though."

Maura tossed her purse over a chair. "Jeeze Louise, Allie. You're a looloo, and the hair suits you. It's a very popular cut. Besides, you'll always have a great rack. No haircut can take that away from you."

Allison chuffed. "Jenny must have taken one look at me standing next to Lisa and decided right then and there to have me all frumped up. It's unendurable." She poked at Timothy's newspaper. "Honey, what is so fascinating about the news that you can't take a moment to tell me how wrong I am?"

"Eight dead, twenty-two wounded. Jesus Harold Christ."

Edward looked at the article over Timothy's shoulder. "From the bombing?"

Timothy smashed the pages together. "No, Eddie, from the Cubs game. Yes, from that bombing." His face grew suddenly haggard, his eyelids drooping. "They done killed three office clerks and five regular Joes. One of 'em in a goddamned stroller."

Allison bent the clip back and forth, searching for the right position. "Do they know who did it?"

He shook his head. "FBI'll have to find out."

Edward took hold of the paper, searching for the front page. "Why can't the police do it?"

"Are you kidding?" Timothy asked. "Chicago cops're nothing but a bunch of Mick monkeys. Can't even match their socks. They still haven't done figured out who killed the mayor two years back."

"Hey, genius." Allison punched Timothy's shoulder. "I'm Irish."

An involuntary snigger formed on his mouth. "Everyone got themselves some atrocity in the family history. It's nothing to be ashamed of."

She forced the clip into her hair. It pushed down at an odd angle so she tried again, growing more frustrated. "Fiddlesticks! Would you help me, babe? My hair's so tight, I can't get it to stay where it's supposed to."

When Timothy stood, his broad shoulders stretched against his cotton undershirt, leaving the short sleeves misshapen over his biceps. He gently shimmied the fake bauble back and forth until it rested in its proper place. "You're looking good for a boy." He kissed the top of her head.

Maura glanced at Lisa's table. "Where is grandma? She's usually the first one here."

Lisa's heels made hollow clicks on the stage as she walked across the balcony's shadow. Rowan's prediction had been correct. A night of fitful fever dreams led to veins of bloodshot panic sprouting from her flawed irises. The second hand of her watch ticked forward like a timer and her ribs compressed over her stomach, producing shallow, wholly unsatisfying breaths. She poised herself just outside the dressing room, listening to the chit chat of her cast mates.

Nothing from the pre-show routine suggested anything unusual. Maura mashed a nearly unusable nub of lipstick against her mouth and left a cherry kiss on her mirror for luck.

Timothy's mouth rounded over a plum, ripping off half of it in a single bite. "When the big cities burn down, the country'll have all the food. Y'all don't know how to hunt or how to farm. All gonna starve to death."

Edward stumbled about in his nervous little steps, slapping at his cheeks while mangling an array of tongue twisters. "Pad kid poured curd pulled cod. Pad kid perked... Pak did... *Drat*, I had it!"

Allie hid her naked body behind the folding screen, damning imagined fat on her thighs. Everything seemed normal. Lisa quietly settled into her chair and opened the boxes of makeup and jewelry.

Allison stuck her head over the screen. "If Jenny says anything more about the vacation scene, I'm going to have myself a conniption fit. She's been at my throat all week."

Maura strayed over to Lisa's table and pressed her fingers along the jagged sharp ends of the copper necklace. "Allie, if you got something to say to Jenny, you should say it directly to her. I could go for some entertainment today."

"She'd never listen, too busy being right about everything." Allison turned to Lisa's dour face. "I don't mean to talk bad about your sister in front of you, but it has become the stuff of farce. Jenny probably needs a good stiff poke. It might do wonders for her personality."

Lisa rubbed her throbbing temples. "Maybe you could show a little empathy. Opening night is tomorrow. Jenn's scared to death."

"And what of me? You don't think I'm scared? A director is meant to inspire confidence in the actors. She never says anything bad about your performance, not even a suggestion. I did the vacation scene the same way for five weeks. Not a word. Suddenly I'm not doing it *big* enough, whatever that means."

Maura picked up Lisa's smoky-glass ball earrings and twiddled them between her fingers. "They look just like pearls."

She held them against her lobes. "Why don't you wear dangle earrings? Earrings are so precious when they hang low."

Lisa kept her focus on her eyeliner in the mirror. "Because pearl studs are worn by affluent women, and Margaret Hunt is very wealthy."

Maura laid them back on the red silk and pointed at the compact box at the table's corner."Why do you wear the mole? No one can see it."

Lisa looked down at the black speck in the case. "Because *I* know it's there." Her pinkie pressed against the tiny mole and applied it to her cheek. "Just like that, I'm Margaret Hunt."

While the cast readied themselves backstage, the door to the office behind the last row of seats swung open. The handle had slammed into the plaster so many times it now nestled into a slowly growing dent on the wall. Jenny Pluviam waddled her body down the stairs and through the middle aisle, an unlit Beechnut clamped between her teeth. Her head remained tilted down as she walked with hunched shoulders. In a husky, cigarette-worn voice, she called out. "Grizz," the stump at the end of her right arm pointed at him on the stage, "a word."

Grizz rolled up his sleeves, exposing bony forearms. A swear came from under his breath. "What's the rumpus, my dear?"

"God, Grizzy, where do I start?" Jenny stopped just before the stage, her hand on her hip.

He gave a weary smile. "Beginning's the best place. That's

where most things start."

She moved up the three short steps on the stage to the ladder behind the balcony. Her foot pushed against the second rung, causing it to creak.

Grizz nodded. "I said I would replace the ladder. It'll be done tonight."

"It still squeaks when they climb up."

"I said—"

"You said you'd take care of it a week ago. Opening night is tomorrow. It would have been nice for Lisa and Eddie to rehearse with the actual ladder they're going to use during the play."

Grizz ground his bent teeth. "Yes, ma'am."

"It has to be silent and safe. Mostly silent. We're still missing three shelves worth of books from behind the sofa—"

"The books are at my apartment, I'll bring them tonight too."

"—and for God's sake, fix that chair at the dining table. Maura can't sit down for her scene. I realize you know jack shit about acting, but imagine trying to perform, worried about falling on your heater."

Grizz pulled a Chesterfield from the breast pocket of his flannel shirt. "Yeah, that'd be rough."

"We're behind the eight ball." Jenny pinched his leathery cheek. "Please, tell me everything's going to be okay, Grizzy."

He lit his cigarette. "We're all ducky. Anything else?"

"Yes, Lisa's light. We'll talk about it when the cattle come." Jenny screamed, her voice ringing throughout the theater. "Actors, time to play!"

All the makeup was applied, the costumes donned, and the accessories added. The five actors came down the wing and reconvened on the stage. And now, there were seven: Lisa, Jenny, Allison, Timothy, Edward, Maura, and Grizz. One of them had planned the perfect murder.

A thick silence, built from anticipation, overtook the theater. The cast stood across the middle of the stage, facing their director in the front row. Jenny said, "Congratulations. You made it to the last rehearsal. I wasn't so sure we would survive. Today is a great day for you but a sad one for me. It's the last day I get to boss you around. You see, once opening night rolls around, the play no longer belongs to the director or the writer, it belongs to the actors. I'm confident it's being left in capable hands. So, one last rodeo." She took a long drag and then crushed the Beechnut under her shoe. "First off, I want to see everyone using their ears this morning. We will be listening to each other on stage. Sometimes we don't do that. Sometimes we just wait for the other person to stop talking. The game is simple, action and reaction. Timothy—"

"Ahh, shit."

"Stop waiting for a laugh. You might not get one from the audience and you can't just stand there like a dope on a rope waiting for something that isn't coming. I don't understand why you're trying to time audience reactions during rehearsal when we don't have an audience. Not too bright, is it?"

"I'm practicing. I don't want them to miss my next line cause they're laughing. That love-letter scene, during the preview, the critics didn't hear dang near half of it."

"You can fart around all day with the pencil, crossing stuff out, scribbling on another sheet, there are any number of things you can do if the audience gets too loud. What you can't do is plan a pause between every line. You only began doing it this week, and it's pissing me off. Speaking of newly acquired blunders—"

Edward covered his face. "I'm sorry." He shook his head. "The worst part is I don't even know I'm doing it."

"Just find your light, Eddie. It's not hard. It's that shiny thing right in front of you. When you talk with Allison about the neighbors, you can walk anywhere near the bookcase, you can even lean on either side. Just stay away from the darkness. And stop hiding yourself in general. You've started looking away from the audience. We want to see your face."

"I got the idea that he's kind of dead. I'm almost playing a shadow."

She put her stump in the air. "Stop with the ideas. Great performances have nothing to do with thinking. While we're on the subject of that scene—"

Allison balled her hands into fists. Her mouth crumpled.

"Allie, my dear Allie, don't give in to Edward when he cancels your vacation. If you do, he's got nowhere to go. He needs you to put up a fight. The last few rehearsals, you've treated it as a mild inconvenience. It needs to be bigger."

Edward raised his hand like a student. "I'm fine in the scene. I have no problem with how Allie does it."

Allison bowed her head. "Thank you, Eddie."

"Yeah, but I have a problem with it. I'm in the audience thinking, *Why doesn't he leave this bitch sooner? She doesn't seem to care.* Don't do that to your character, Allie. Give her some integrity."

Allison gave the barest hint of assent.

"Grizz, don't bring up Lisa's light on the balcony until she moves forward. Only Edward is lit at the start and then after his cue...What's the cue Edward?"

"*Is someone there.*"

Jenny nodded. "Right. After Edward says that line, then, and only then do you bring up Lisa's light. Any questions?"

Edward raised his hand. "Lisa's light shines right in my eyes on the balcony. I can't see anything."

"You don't need to see anything. Just don't fall. Any other questions?"

Maura said, "What about jewelry?"

Jenny did a double take. "I...I don't know, Maura. What *about* jewelry?"

"I know I'm supposed to be sixteen, but I know for a fact that sixteen-year-olds wear jewelry. Allie gets to wear that ugly thing in her hair and Lisa's decked out to the nines. Can't I wear something nice?"

"By something nice, I presume you mean something ostentatious?"

Maura scrunched her face. "I don't know that company. I like Monocraft. A brooch with my initials maybe."

"I'll get right on that. It might take a few months. Any *relevant* questions?"

Allison said, "Do you have any notes for Lisa?"

"For Lisa?" Jenny sighed.

"You must have something to say about her. She's the lead role after all."

"Hey sis?"

Lisa raised her head. "Yeah, Jenn."

"Don't change what you're doing."

Lisa grinned. "Don't you think I know that?"

Jenny stared right through Allison as she spoke. "Lisa gets plenty of notes from me when we're at home. Worry about your performance, not hers. All right, actors to your places. Let's do it right so we can all go home and read the funny papers."

At the back of the theater, Christine wobbled, hands planted on the seat in front of her with a white-knuckle grip. "That voice. Where have I heard that voice? I must remember."

3

JUST A COINCIDENCE

12:20 p.m. Thursday, April 4th

"Con job." Sergeant Grady sipped his beer.

Rowan lit one of his inevitable cigarettes. "What is the con? What could be gained by hiring a detective?"

Grady had a white walrus mustache he refused to take care of. The liquor coated the lower hairs, so he constantly cleaned them with a wipe of his wrist. His advancing years had produced bruised hollows under his eyes, a look of defeat permanently fixed to his face. His voice rasped like burnt sandpaper. "Doesn't matter, you walk away."

The two men sat in the middle of the otherwise empty Brown

Bear Bar, permeated with the previous night's mephitic odor of alcohol, tobacco, sweat, and the vomit-inducing lemon cologne favored by the patrons. Mottled light sprayed through the dusty window, filtering through snaking lines of stagnant smoke and coating the room with a bluish hue.

Rowan's table bordered the platform supporting the eponymous, stuffed brown bear. The bartender, Dave Bowen, always kept the table vacated, should his favorite customer ever want a drink. "I have already given her my word. I cannot back out now."

"What's the woman's name again?" asked Grady.

"Lisa Pluviam."

"Pluviam...Pluviam...It sounds familiar."

"She was in a play last year."

"Do I look like I go to the theater?"

"Perhaps you have read her name in the paper," Rowan suggested.

"I don't read the paper. Too depressing. Hold up." Grady shouted over to the bar. "Hey Bowen, did you put up those missing-person flyers like I asked?"

Dave Bowen slapped a rag over the brass pump. "Come on, Grady."

The sergeant simpered under his mustache. "Where we going? Are we going to see the health inspector? How about the Liquor Control Commission?"

Dave pleaded with him. "People come here to escape

depression, not to look at a bunch of missing people. You think they're going to wake up hung over the next morning and form a search party? Most of my patrons can't remember anything from the night before. The flyers just make the place look ugly."

"Too late." Grady pointed a crooked finger. "If those flyers lead to even one person found, it'll be worth having them on your wall. I asked you nicely a week ago. Today, I'm telling you."

"But I have a theme going."

"Theme? Don't bump gums with me. You're called The Brown Bear. What's this next to me? A big, fucking brown bear. Theme accomplished."

Dave threw his arms into the air. "Fine. They're spooky, all right? I don't like looking at them. Every time I turned to the wall, there they were, staring at me with those goddamn smiles on their faces. Meanwhile, I know exactly where they are. They're in shallow graves or riverbeds. And not one of them is smiling. A couple of them have been missing for twenty years. Hell, one guy is almost my age by now. He's either dead or he doesn't want to be found."

"Get those flyers back on the wall by tomorrow!" Grady turned back to Rowan. "That cocksucker. What were we talking about?"

"Lisa Pluviam."

"Right, right. She has no idea who left the note?"

"Not the slightest inkling."

Grady shrugged. "If the woman won't report it, she must not

think too much of it. Most threats never amount to anything. You know that. Why threaten somebody when you could kill them without all the paperwork? But just for a lark, let's say you thought someone was going to kill you on a certain day, during a certain time, at a certain place. What's the first thing you'd make sure not to do?"

Rowan grimaced. "She has reasons. They are not logical ones, but I believe she—"

"Hey Einstein, what's the first thing you'd make sure not to do?"

"Show up," he said glumly.

"Ring-a-ding-ding, we have a winner. All this malarkey about how the show must go on."

He is right. I know he is. But... "She is a friend, and I would like to be certain."

Grady gave his best impression of a smile. "What do you want me to say?"

"I called you because I wanted your advice."

"Bull. You called me because you wanted me to tell you it was a great idea. Well, it's not." Grady sighed. "On the other hand, it couldn't hurt to just go there and watch her. Be prepared for some tomfoolery though. Actors." He retched. "Bunch of grownups playing make-believe. Think they're so damned important. Do they ever get killed in the line of duty?" He jabbed at Rowan's shoulder. "Hey, I guess you'll find out the answer to that question tomorrow, huh?"

Rowan gave a forced, little cough. "Williams will be backstage, and I will be in the audience. We could use someone at the entrance. I know you have got a lot on your plate."

Grady gibbered an unbroken line of swears and then immediately apologized. "I'm not mad at you, son."

He still calls me son. "The bombing?"

A pained look appeared on his face as he nodded. "Yeah, what the hell's wrong with this city. I hope they get taken alive. It'd be worth it to catch them alive just to fry them on the hotsquat later."

"Any leads?"

"We only know that the bastards used pyrotol. Not much to go on. The feds arrive tomorrow morning, and I'm going to look like a dumb bag of shit."

Rowan squeezed the charred tip of his cigarette onto the floor. "Where would pyrotol be obtained?"

"Nowhere. They stopped producing it. After the war, the government sold all the reserves. It went fast."

"What is its primary purpose?"

"Blowing out tree stumps and clearing ditches. Some maniac used it to blow up a school in Massachusetts a few years back. Occasionally, it was used in government projects, building bridges and such."

"Can sales in Illinois be traced?" asked Rowan.

"We're trying." Grady checked his watch, slammed back the rest of his beer, and licked his mustache. "Time to skedaddle. The commies are marching today. They spout their nonsense, a crowd gathers, and before you know it, we have a moving riot on our hands. God knows how many arrests by the end of the day."

"The entrance?"

"I can spare one cop. And he won't be competent in any way. Name's Young."

"Thank you, Grady."

"The guy's a real fuck-up. He'll probably do more harm than good."

"I appreciate it."

A sea of red marched down Ashland, monstrous draping banners of hammers and sickles hoisted every twenty feet. The protesters shouted their chants in perfectly timed unison. "The proletarians have nothing to lose but their chains!"

Maura pressed her hands against the dash as she blew an enormous bulb of a bubble. It made a loud, bright pop before it deflated over her cherry lips. "What are proletarians?"

Edward's legs twisted about with cramped muscles. For the fifth time in the last minute, he grabbed the rearview mirror, adjusting it before settling it back in its original position. "I think they're meant to be us. Are you all right back there, Christine? Is it too hot for you?"

The sunlight drenched the back seat of the Auburn sedan with heavy, stifling rays. Christine's frizzy white hair, which had been standing on end, was now bent down on one side from sweat. She rubbed her lobes. "I'm a bit sore, dear. Why are we stopped?"

"A protest."

Maura grabbed hold of the headrest with both hands. "Did you like the play, Miss Filius?"

"Oh, yes. Edward was magnificent. Though I must say, I don't like him on that balcony. It looked terribly unsafe."

"We're professionals." She winked at Edward. "Ain't we, Eddie?"

He looked down to her nyloned knee.

"You and Christine live together?" asked Maura.

"Christine needs daily care, so I have to live with her. She doesn't have anyone else. I've seen the inside of those shelters. Gosh darn awful—"

Maura cut him off. "So, the answer is *yes*?"

"Yes, we live together."

"What about your parents? Where are they?"

"Both dead. Well, my mother is dead. My father, I'm not sure."

"Is this a sore subject?" Maura asked. "You can tell me to zip it. I won't get offended."

The march continued in front of them with no sign of the tail end. "No. My mother died of..." Edward looked back to the mirror. "Christine, what did Mom die of?"

"She was shot by an Italian. An ugly one."

"No, *my* mom. Your sister. What did she die of?"

Christine crinkled her forehead in thought. "Oh, it was sepsis. She died at the hospital after you were born. Quite painful as I

49

recall."

Maura smiled. "That's a good mom."

Edward looked at her with disbelief. "Dying from sepsis makes you a good mom?"

"Acksherly, it does."

"Ac*tually*. It's pronounced ac*tually*."

"Think about it. She died giving birth to you. I wish my mom died giving birth to me. It would be the first good thing she did in her life."

"No, it was well after I was born. Mom was sick. Plum loco in la cabeza."

"What about your dad?"

Edward frowned. "I never knew him. He left her for another woman, then skipped town."

"I never knew my dad either, died before I was born. That's kinda crazy. Allison grew up with no dad or mom. And Tim, his mom died when he was a baby. We're all a buncha guttersnipes."

The chant in the streets changed to *Justice for Abe Gray*. Maura turned to Edward, propping her knees onto the seat. "You know something funny, I got only one photo of my dad. He's standing in front of an iron mill, with a gigantic shovel held across his waist. And he's got those glasses, those funny-looking protective glasses. So's when I dream about him, he always looks like that. It must be cause it's the only way I've ever seen him. In the dreams, I always tell him to take off the glasses cause I want to see his eyes. He never does. Isn't that creepy?"

Christine reached from the back seat, laying her hand on Edward's shoulder. "Dear, I'm feeling a bit faint. Could you drive under some shade?"

Edward jabbed the steering wheel. "I can't drive anywhere." Buried at the front of the small crowd gathered on the sidewalk, a police uniform flashed in Edward's line of sight. "Wait here, you two. I'll see if that cop knows how long it's going to be." He exited the car, crossing the street and jostling through the gawking public.

Maura stretched out the gum with her fingers and pulled it back into her mouth one chomp at a time. "What about me, Miss Filius? Was I a believable teenager?"

Christine's stuttered, her head turning back and forth as if she were searching the car. "Where is Edward? Who are you?"

"I'm Eddie's friend. You and I have been talking the whole car ride."

Her upper lip curled. "Oh, yes. I recognized your voice."

A smile slashed across Maura's face. "Did you, now?"

"You had changed your hair. That's why I didn't recognize you. Now I remember. You were the one in the attic."

"Acksherly, I've never been in your attic and my hair has been this way since I saw *The Canary Murder Case* in the cinema. Do you know Louise Brooks? Everyone says I look like her."

"Are you taking the test?"

Maura sputtered out a laugh. "I think you need a nap, Miss Filius." She looked down at the two white, cardboard boxes next to Christine and then back to the old woman's vacant eyes.

Edward returned a few minutes later, restarting the car and slowly going back and forth in an effort to turn round. "The cop told me this march is headed to the meat packing plant. We can get through at Fulton. Should be clear all the way to the hospital." The car finally finished its tortured u-turn. "No worries, Christine. We're on the move."

Nurse Gonzalez was filing her nails at the hospital reception desk, the sound of her jangling bracelet producing a sterile, tinkling echo in the white room. "So when's the first show?"

Edward set the boxes in front of her. "Tomorrow night."

"I hope I can come next week, but you know, people keep getting sick and dying."

"Nice. Well, *that's* not nice, but I hope you can make it."

The nurse pulled out a form from the filing cabinet. "Are you nervous? I couldn't stand all those people watching me."

"I won't know 'til I get up there and say my lines."

"Don't you have to imagine them all naked? Isn't that what you're supposed to do?"

"No." Edward looked back at the car through the glass door. Maura was leaning across to the back seat. "Lisa told me to pretend they aren't there. That way it's just you on stage alone."

"Who's Lisa?"

"She's one of the actresses," Edward said, still looking at the car outside.

The nurse squinted at the paper taped to the box. "Eddie, be a dear and read off those formulas for me. My eyes have gone to pot, and I forgot my glasses at home."

He opened the flaps of the top box and pulled out a bottle. "C-seventeen, H-nineteen, N, O-three."

"C-seventeen, H-nineteen, N, O-three. Got it. And the other one?"

"C-thirty-seven, H-forty two, Cl—" He stopped. Maura was standing outside the car now, a look of horror on her face. Edward's legs moved slowly at first, but then faster through the door. The nurse's voice called out to him in a distant, faded drone as he ran across the short sidewalk onto the asphalt. Christine's body was bent over at the waist. The eyes were open, but no breath was coming from her mouth. Maura finally let loose with a scream. A pair of orderlies wheeled out a gurney, and they all made a mad rush to the emergency ward.

Nurse Gonzalez caught Edward's arm at the emergency doors, yanking him against the wall. "I'm sorry, Eddie. You have to stay out here."

Rowan pushed and pulled on the front rail. The wood nudged a bit in either direction but not enough to suggest sabotage. It was disappointing but not surprising. Although the ladder could be made rickety and the railing unscrewed a bit in strategic places, one could be prepared for those things. Even a brazen murderer would surely eschew such methods.

Walter looked out over the two-hundred seats. "More than likely, the attempt will happen backstage. Don't you think?"

Walter's reasoning was sound. Visibility was a key issue in the construction of this would-be crime. A murder committed in front of that many witnesses wouldn't imply braggadocio as much as blinding insanity. Yet, the opened script was the kind of clue that gnawed at Rowan, and the balcony stood out as the most obviously dangerous place in the theater. "Edward will be on the other side of this partition. Go over and attempt to reach me."

Walter walked a few feet toward the ladder, crossing onto the other half of the balcony. Careful not to disturb the many potted flowers, he leaned over the rail, barely hooking Rowan's wide lapel between two outstretched fingers. "I can do it, but it's not a solid grip. If Edward had a long knife, he could reach over and stab her, but no matter what he does, everyone in the auditorium will be able to see it."

"Yes, we continue to encounter the problem of the audience. Perhaps the killer is counting on them seeing what they expect rather than the actual event. Does Edward ever touch her in this scene? Even holding hands?"

"No, not here. He doesn't make physical contact until act two when she visits his apartment and they kiss. I know you've got it in your mind that this is the scene, but you're on the wrong track. Finding the death threat on this page of the script was probably just a coincidence."

"It does not feel coincidental. But, perhaps in your own tangential, confused way, you are on to something. We should focus more on Lisa's movement *throughout* the play." Rowan paced the short platform. "So, my friend, from the top. The lights come up on scene one. Where is she?"

Walter pulled his notebook from the inside of his suit coat. "We all start in the dressing room. When it's show time, Timothy and Lisa go through the wing to the crossover and wait for their cue. They enter at the right slit in the curtain to the dining room."

"Is that stage right or house right?"

He paused for a moment and then pointed.

Rowan said, "That is stage left. Use the lingo."

Walter made a note of it. "Gotcha. So they enter stage left. At some point, Maura comes to the crossover and enters the same way. They fight, they tell each other off. The lights go down and all three actors exit and return to the dressing room."

"Scene two is with Allison and Edward?" asked Rowan.

"Affirmative. It's about fifteen pages long. Awful stuff. It makes scene one sound like Dashiell Hammett. While that's happening, Timothy and Maura head to the crossover to get ready for their scene three entrance. I'll be alone with Lisa in the dressing room the whole time. When the second scene mercifully ends, Maura and Timothy get on stage for scene three. She's going to run away from home and her father begs her to stay."

"Concentrate, Williams. I do not care about the play. When and where does Lisa move?"

"Lisa and I are in the dressing room for scenes two and three. The balcony is scene four. Lisa and Edward wait in the crossover behind the..." Walter checked his notes. "...stage right side of the curtain. This slit." He pointed down to the stage directly behind them. "After scene three ends, Edward comes up the ladder first and then Lisa follows. He comes forward to the railing and has a monologue. It's not really a monologue though. He talks to these flowers about the sun and the moon—"

Rowan made a cranking motion with his hand.

"Right, right. Lisa waits at the back near the ladder."

Rowan walked to the back of the balcony. "In total darkness?"

"Yes. Edward says his cue, *Is someone there?* After that line, Lisa comes forward and joins him. Lights up on her, and they have dialogue. *Oh fancy meeting you, I'm your neighbor, blah blah blah.* When the scene ends, they climb down the ladder. Edward goes back to the dressing room, but Lisa remains onstage and walks to the dining table where she's joined by Timothy and Allison for scene five. After the fifth scene, act one is over and we have an intermission."

"This is where it will happen. She is alone and enshrouded by darkness."

"How?" Walter knocked on the partition. "Edward has the wall between him and Lisa. I'm watching the ladder the whole time. No one can get up here. I figure no one can touch her."

Rowan pointed to the catwalk. "That spot provides a propitious opportunity."

"That's ten feet away. What would Grizz do from there? Shoot her? He'd be arrested immediately. I still say we're looking backstage. That is, if we're looking at all."

Rowan grimaced. "Do you want to go home, Williams? I can handle this assignment without you just fine."

Walter sighed. "Manory, you know I'm not leaving you alone."

"Then no more baseless innuendo. Let's hear the movements of acts two and three."

The detectives finished hashing over the rest of the plot without making much headway as to the killer's method. While Walter checked the exits, Rowan shuffled up the iron staircase to Lisa's office. She was leaning back in the chair with her legs propped up on the desk. Rowan's eyes drifted from her exposed thigh above knee-high, polka dot socks, past the emerald lamp shade, and finally settled on the pack of Chesterfields jammed at the base of the Underwood. "Walter will be finished in a few minutes. We will not keep you much longer."

Lisa said, "You were right."

"About what?"

"I can't stop thinking about the note." She tied her hair into a lazy bun, a single black lock falling demurely over her face.

How do women do that? They must practice for hours.

"And the more I think about it, the more I realize it's not a joke. They had to spend time cutting out the letters, gluing it together and then sneaking it into my office. It's too much effort, isn't it?"

"Was there anything out of the ordinary during today's rehearsal? Anything at all?"

"Not really. We rehearsed the same as always."

Rowan nodded. *What if Grady and Walter are right? If there is something you are hiding, Lisa, now would be the time to tell me.*

She stood, turning off the desk lamp. "You look troubled."

He motioned toward her desk. "I thought you did not smoke."

"I don't."

Rowan pointed to the Chesterfields under the typewriter.

"Oh, those." She slid them into the drawer. "Grizz's. He must have left them here."

Maura brought Edward a Styrofoam cup of burnt hospital coffee with the dregs forming a layer of sludge at the bottom. He grasped it with shaky hands and tilted the cup forward, scalding his lips. "She's been in there a long time. It must've come out one way or the other by now, don't you think?"

Maura tried to fill the cold waiting room with positivity, remarking how lucky they had been, being at a hospital and deciding not to wait for the march to pass. None of it eased Edward in the slightest.

"I knew something was wrong. You never think about how you'll move on after they die. It never occurs to you. She's the only constant thing I've—"

A doctor walked through the emergency doors, his head bent toward the clipboard in his hands. There was no emotion on his face, or at least, nothing Edward could read.

He sprang from the sofa. "Is…Is she dead?"

The doctor took a pen to the clipboard, checking something or other. "She's fine, Mr. Filius."

"What do you mean, fine?"

"I mean there is nothing wrong with your aunt. She's absolutely fine."

A pent-up breath rushed free from Edward's mouth. "Oh, thank God." He laid his hand over his breast and laughed.

Maura put her head on his shoulder. "See, Eddie. I told you everything would be okay."

"I can't tell you how extraordinary this is," said the doctor with raised eyebrows. "Resuscitation failed, but there was still a faint heartbeat. We are one of the few hospitals in Chicago equipped with an iron lung. I made the decision to encase her, and she responded quite well. We were determining the next course of action when there came a knocking on the glass. Never seen anything like it. Did she show any symptoms at all?"

Edward looked to Maura.

She said, "No. Nothing. One minute she was there and then the lights went out."

Edward said, "That's not quite accurate. She had been a little less communicative today. And she was complaining of heat."

The doctor made a note. "Well, she's a little batty, but her vitals are positively humming. Very strong."

"Batty's good. Batty's normal. Can I take her home?"

"We'd like to keep her a few more days, just for observation."

"Whatever you say, but I'll need to get her personables. Her purse and her jewelry."

"Nurse Gonzalez has them. You can collect at the front desk."

Edward thanked the doctor a few times before heading for the exit with Maura by his side. "I'm sorry, Maura. I'm not in much of a mood for the shindig. I guess this was a disappointing date."

"Aww, don't get all sweaty about it. We'll go next week with Allie and Tim. I should get home anyway what with the play tomorrow and everything."

"Can I at least give you a ride?"

She shook her head. "I'll walk."

"That's silly. Let me drive you. It's getting late."

"No, I like walking. See you tomorrow, Eddie."

He stopped at the desk and called out to her. "Hey, Maura."

"Yeah?" she said from the doorway.

"Did she say anything? You know, before she passed out?"

"I hate to say it, Eddie, but she's a full-blown whackaloon. Nothing she said made any sense."

"Tell me anyway. Please."

"She kept going on about taking a test."

Edward nodded. "She used to be a teacher. Maybe she was remembering something from the past."

"She also told me to stay out of the attic. Do you even have an attic in your house?"

"Yeah, but we don't go up there."

4

OPENING NIGHT

Rowan sat in the chair, concentrating on the task of rolling a tidy cigarette. Grizz offered him a Chesterfield. "No, thank you. I find that commercial cigarettes taste of dust."

Jenny sat, smoking behind her desk, her heft creaking the wood of the chair. "Forgive me if I'm in a foul mood, detective. I just learned of this situation last night. Lisa has quite the talent for creating turmoil at the last minute." She threw her pack to the edge of the table. "Join the party, Walter."

Walter scrunched up his face. "Manory smokes enough for the both of us." He hovered over the pack on the desk. "Beechnuts?

Aren't those men's cigarettes?"

"Isn't that the same pansy bowtie Marlene Dietrich wore in *Morocco*?"

He nodded. "Touché, Miss Pluviam. Touché."

Rowan's exhalant smoke mingled with the cloud in the center of the room. "I'm curious. As the director, you have firsthand knowledge of the respective personalities of the cast. Do you have any theories about who is behind this threat?"

"Oh, yeah. Sure."

He waited. The second hand of the clock on the wall ticked six times. "Care to share them with me?"

"Not especially," Jenny said flippantly.

"Now I *am* curious."

"I'm not going to share my thoughts with you because of the cop you got back there. Lying can lead to jail if the police are involved, and my sister is my lead actress."

Rowan put two and two together. "You believe your sister concocted this story?"

Jenny finally smiled. "I didn't say that out loud. You did. Who knows, it might be true."

"If you had to guess?"

Her eyes shifted to the tip of her cigarette as if she were studying it. "I don't have to guess. That sounds an awful lot like your job."

Rowan pointed at Grizz. "And you? Any theories?"

With arms folded, Grizz leaned against the wall behind Jenny, the cigarette stuck to his chapped lower lip. "It was Maura that done it."

"Miss Lewis? Did you see her entering Lisa's office?"

"No, but she's one o' them starry-eyed types. I can see her getting it in her head to scare Lisa away—take the role for herself. Or it coulda been Edward. Why did he audition? Never did a play before and all the sudden he wants to be an actor. My foot. Maybe he did it to get closer to Lisa. Or maybe—"

Jenny said, "You're done in here, Grizzy. I don't need you anymore. Go make sure Eddie's tape is in the right place so he doesn't wander off the stage."

Rowan could swear he heard a certain four-letter word muttered under Grizz's breath as he left. He made a steeple of his fingers. "If this is all a farce, why do you think she hired me?"

Jenny stubbed out her cigarette. "Lisa is my sister. If she feels that she needs protection, I'm happy to have you here. It doesn't matter what I think. Just don't disrupt my play and for God's sake—"

"What happened to your hand?"

"Excuse me?"

"You heard my question just fine."

Jenny snorted. "Accident."

"I stubbed my toe this morning. That was an accident."

"A *bad* accident."

"Merely engaging in small talk. If you do not wish to discuss it..."

"My hand was run over by a car many years ago in New York. Is it pertinent to your job?"

Rowan leaned forward. "That depends. What were you doing in New York?"

"The same thing you're doing now."

"Which is?"

"Fishing." Jenny pointed her stump at the door. "If you'll excuse me, I have a lot of work to do, and none of it involves your questions."

"Of course. Come, Williams." They ran down the iron staircase into the aisle. "Did you see that? She wanted out of that conversation faster than the Nazis wanted out of the Sturmabteilung."

Walter said, "I don't speak German."

"She is hiding something." Rowan checked his pocket watch. "The actors will be arriving soon. Lisa will inform them about the threat when they are all gathered in the dressing room. Then I will address them personally."

"Manory?"

"Yes?"

"What do you think it's like to bed an amputee?"

"Stop talking."

"But—"

"Just stop."

"We'll discuss it later. Oh, here. I grabbed you a program from the front of house."

Stuffing it lazily inside his suit pocket, Rowan looked back to the window of Lisa's office. *Why would she hire me if she is lying?*

The cast listened, first with curiosity, then almost impassively, and finally, with stunned clarity. A stagnant, funereal atmosphere hung in the dry air of the dressing room. They sat on chairs, surrounding Lisa in a frightened little bundle. Rowan stood with his back to the wall, studying the reactions, trying to gauge if any of them were capable. *To a man, they all seem surprised.*

Lisa's voice could not disguise her apprehension. "We have to act as if nothing is wrong. These past weeks have been so wonderful, I hate to introduce this…this ghastly distraction."

Timothy was the first to speak. "We gotta cancel the play."

Allison glared at him. "It's Lisa's decision."

"Horseshit. I don't care what she wants to do."

"Babe, what if it's not real? What if we cancel the play for no reason at all? Think of all the work we've put into it." Allison turned to Lisa. "She's a big girl. She can decide for herself."

Edward looked sick, his eyes unfocused. "It can't be real. It's got to be a joke, right?"

Timothy walked aimless circles. His nails dug into his palms. "A very unfunny one. You got no idea who it is, Leece?"

She answered by lowering her head.

Edward kept going, talking to no one in particular. "How could he hope to get away with it? Two-hundred people will be watching."

"What do you mean *he*?" Timothy folded his arms. "It could be a woman. We don't know."

Maura pressed her hand across her chest. "Well, it isn't me. I've been with myself all day, and I didn't plan a murder. I have trouble planning dinner. And who's to say it's somebody in this room? Grizz and Jenny were here on Wednesday. You're all acting like it's got to be one of us."

Edward looked around at the faces of his cast mates. "No one in this room would kill anyone. The very idea is absurd. But I must say, I feel the same about Jenn and Grizz. I just can't imagine anyone doing something like this."

Timothy finally settled against the dresser. "Even if I was some maniac killer, I wouldn't be right stupid enough to tell everybody what I was going to do. When did you get it, Leece?"

Lisa was about to answer when Rowan butted in. "It is not necessary for you to know that."

"Why is that? Who the hell are you people anyway? Are you cops?"

Rowan thought one of them might slip up and say something they shouldn't have known. It was a technique he had used successfully many times; the less information the suspects had, the more likely the killer among them would foolishly reveal his true nature. Rowan introduced himself along with Walter and Officer Young. Then, in the midst of the room's grimness, he decided to extend an olive branch, recommending that, if anyone had made a miscalculated attempt at humor, he or she could cop to it now and face no repercussions. As he fully expected, no one copped.

"Then it is my duty to inform you, or at least one of you, that there is no hope of escape if you are preposterous enough to attempt to make good on this vile threat. Not only will I be watching everything on the stage, and not only will a police officer be stationed at the entrance, but my trusted assistant will be following Miss Pluviam backstage at all times. We have eyes everywhere. There will be no murder tonight." He pulled Young aside to give him more specific instructions.

Walter took this opportunity to warm himself to the cast. "I want all of you to know that I will do my best to stay out of your way and not interfere with your performance. Pretend I'm not here. On a personal note, I know the situation seems dire, but Manory and I are professionals. We are quite confident you will all make it through tonight unscathed."

Maura tugged on his sleeve. "Walt?"

"Yes, my dear?"

"Does this mean all of our lives are in danger? I mean, a guy who's slap-happy, he's not going to care who gets killed."

"Nothing will happen to you. Not while I'm around."

Rowan said, "Williams." Walter and Maura turned to him. It was then that the detective got a centered view of the girl and saw something odd, something he hadn't expected. He saw recognition in her face. "Let us continue our inspection of the theater. We'll give the actors some privacy." Officer Young remained housed in the wing, just outside the door.

Forty-five minutes before show time, Lisa stepped into her ankle-length silver gown. She put on her necklace and earrings. Her hand touched the reflection of her mole. "Goodbye, Lisa Pluviam. Hello, Margaret Hunt."

A line formed outside the door, soon running up and around the block. Wealthy theatergoers chatted away about the positive reviews and worried about the cast of unknowns, except for that Lisa Pluviam woman who had been so fine in that play they couldn't remember the name of. A female director was such an eccentric strategy, and surely the drama would be a far more emotional experience, but perhaps a bit technically deficient.

At twenty to seven, they were admitted into the red velvet maze of the front of house, past the ticket booth, and through the candle-lit hallway, scarcely noticing the shadowed policeman eyeing them as they entered.

The entire stage was lit with each of the three sections displaying their designated lighting scheme. The dining room at the right had a rather harsh glare bouncing off the plates and silverware. The sofa and bookcase in the middle appeared quite comfortable due to some thick gauze. The balcony was lit with a filtered, pale light, creating weak, nearly transparent shadows.

Grizz stood at his position on the catwalk. Jenny leaned on the iron rail in front of her office. The actors were ready backstage. Walter stood by Lisa and Timothy's side in the crossover. Rowan knelt next to the first row and lit a cigarette. *The Balcony* was ready to begin.

As the lights went down, a hush overcame the auditorium. For a few seconds, the world was black and then...

The audience burst into applause when the dining table was lit. Lisa entered with Timothy following behind her. Peeking through the sliver of the curtain, Walter watched the drama unfold.

Timothy began the play, his country accent vanished.

I don't see how you can be disappointed by roses. They are the most accepted and sought after flowers in the world. Everyone from kings and queens down to your mother thinks they are marvelous.

It isn't the type of flower, my dear. It's the color. Red suggests passion. It would be unseemly for me to present them to your employer unless you want me to make an advance. Yellow would have been a far more tasteful option. Anyway, they're half-dead.

I'm half-dead myself, matter of fact. I had to go right down to Michigan Avenue...

You've only been gone twenty minutes.

I ran into our neighbors. They recognized me and offered me a lift. I say, the wife is a smasher.

How many times have you been warned about discussing another woman in front of me?

Maura crept into the crossover and tapped Walter on the shoulder. He whirled around like a panicked child. "Don't scare me like that." She gave a silent cackle and put on an extra coat of lipstick.

Caught them necking in her room. Most unbecoming.

As long as it's relegated to the neck and above.

Where is that girl? Lana?

Maura poked Walter again. "Walter, do you want to hear a good joke?"

"Isn't that your cue?"

Lana!

"How do you get Jenny Pluviam to fall from a tree?"

"I don't know."

"You wave to her." She slipped through the curtain. Another wild round of applause greeted her entrance.

Rowan crouched at the corner of the stage, rivulets of sweat curving down his pale cheeks. His hands and feet grew numb. The more he tried to slow his breath, the faster his heart beat against his chest. Where was it going to come from? How long until the balcony scene?

Daddy leaves whenever he tires of you and whenever he fears me. Perhaps if he grew a backbone and you had any sense of fun, we'd have him round the house more often.

Laura, sweetie, I'm not afraid of you. I'll have you know I killed several Krauts during the war.

A minute before the scene was to end, Edward and Allison came through the wing to the crossover. She peeked through the slit. "Timmy's dying out there. He's lost."

Edward squeezed her hand. "The only thing we can do is focus on our scene. Timothy will get it together." He leaned toward Walter. "Anything strange?"

"No, but we have a long way to go."

The lights faded on the first scene and, with the applause booming behind them, Walter and Lisa trailed Maura and Timothy down the wing into the dressing room. Maura kicked the folding screen, knocking it sideways. "Come on, Tim! My name is Lana, not Laura."

He combed his hair with his fingers. "I'm sorry. I got Maura in my head and then I remembered Lana and they done got mixed together."

"Lisa called me Lana, you call me Laura. What's my damn

71

name?"

Lisa put her arm around Tim. "Enough, Maura. It's just a small mistake. He's supposed to be forgetful anyway. Are you okay, Tim? You seem preoccupied."

"Of course I'm preoccupied. What's gonna happen to you, Leece?"

She wrapped her hands around the side of his face. "I can take care of myself, Tim. Don't worry about me."

Maura threw her arms in the air. "Some of us are trying to put on a play." She stomped down the wing with a huff.

Walter gave Timothy a sympathetic pat on the back. "You'd better go with her, son. Lisa will be safe with me."

Timothy gave one last look to Lisa before dropping his head, and slumping down the wing after Maura.

Walter waited a few seconds to make sure he was out of earshot. "Christ almighty, he didn't just screw up the name. That man rewrote significant portions of the play. I met Jenny; she's going to have Tim's ass for dinner."

"That was a horrible start." Lisa collapsed in the chair, her head stuffed into her hands. "Can you get me a glass of water, Walter?"

He pulled a cup from the little cupboard above the chest of drawers and ran some tap water through the groaning pipes. "Feeling rough?"

"Headache. Only two more scenes before the balcony. That's when Rowan thinks it's going to happen. He may be right."

"He's been wrong once or twice."

Rowan shuffled down the hall to the front of house. With Allison and Edward on stage, he thought it a good time to check in with Officer Young. "Anything suspicious?"

Young was smoking and chatting up Horus, the house manager. "A few homelesses staring through the windows. Other than that, nothing."

"Good. Be alert."

Young tipped his cap and smiled. "The world needs more lerts."

"Amusing." *Idiot.*

Back on stage, Allison was lounging on the sofa with her feet dangling over the edge.

Carey, you're just plain confused. Goodnight Irene is a song.

No, it isn't, darling. It's a book. A dreadful book filled with even more dreadful murder. Couldn't read a word of it.

That's true, but it was a song first. Don't be so daft.

As daft as our neighbor friend, whatsisname?

Ugh. Did you see the flowers he chose? Half dead they were.

I suppose someone has to adopt dying flowers or they'll never escape the florists.

The voices on stage carried through to the dressing room, ghostlike and hollow. Lisa smiled. "They're good together, Allison and Edward."

Walter said, "I've only been around them today, but I had the impression that *Maura* and Edward were good together."

She lifted an eyebrow. "I mean onstage."

"Oh, right. I know much less about that kind of chemistry." He cleared his throat. "By the by, after this is all over and you survive the performance, I think you should give Manory some thought?"

"Some thought?"

"I mean to say that he's available."

Lisa gave a mischievous look without saying anything.

"Why not?"

"I didn't think Rowan was much interested in women if you get my drift. I tried every trick in the book."

"No. Oh, no. He's virile, a real Butch Masterson. He's just a bit socially..." Walter searched for the word. "...inept. He likes you. Trust me."

"I'll keep it in mind, Walter. Thanks for the tip."

Walter bit his tongue. *That's what the prostitute said to the leper.* "No problem."

Scene two came to a close. Allison jumped onto Edward's back and he carried her down the wing. She was beaming when they got to the dressing room. "That was positively ginchy, Eddie.

They loved it."

Edward sighed. "First scene down. Thanks for saving me, Allie. I forgot that line about your dad."

Lisa said, "Sounded great, you two." She stood and took a deep breath. "Ready, Eddie."

Edward took her by the hand, twirled her round, and dipped her. "It's…" He held the pose for a few seconds then pulled her back to a standing position. "I was going to say something clever, but there's nothing that rhymes with Lisa."

Almost apologetically, Walter stepped between them. "You go first, Edward. We'll follow you."

"Of course."

They left Allison alone in the dressing room. She gazed longingly at her reflection. "Everything's going to work out. Timmy will come around. This play is a hit. Even my hair… Oh, shoot. I didn't put my hair clip in." Her hand swept across the table in an effort to find it. "Where did I put it? I have to talk about it in my next scene. Why didn't anyone tell me?" She rifled through the messy pile of silk scarves in the chest of drawers. "Fiddlesticks!"

Sweating under the intensity of the light, Timothy did his best to focus on the scene with Maura.

I'm afraid I do ramble on, Laura—

Lana.

Lana. And then I...

Then you forget...

Yes, of course, I forget what I'm rambling about. I've lost who I am. My identity has done been... And I...I—

Well, never mind, Daddy. If you have to leave, you just leave. I'll find you.

You're awfully good to put up with it like you do. I'm afraid I wouldn't last long without your mother.

You're muddled up, that's all. You imagine things that simply aren't true. That's why I hate leaving you in her clutches. What will become of you?

Edward and Lisa watched the scene unfold through the slit. Walter shadowed them, his eyes darting around the crossover. *There's no way it can happen. Allison and Tim will be back here. Maura in the dressing room. Edward behind the partition. Grizz on the catwalk. And Jenny near the offices.* A faint creaking sound came from behind. *Allison.*

She emerged from the wing's entrance and walked toward them, her expression sour, almost vindictive, and her right hand clasped shut as if it were holding something. Anticipating the worst, Walter moved in front of Lisa with his arms outstretched. Allison called out, "Hey, genius." When Lisa and Edward turned around, Allison went into a cold, confused stupor. The woman was dumbstruck.

Walter whispered loudly. "What are you doing, Allison? You don't go on stage until scene five. Get back to the dressing room."

"Sorry, I...I made a mistake." She fled back through the wing.

Walter made eye contact with the two actors, in search of an explanation, but they both gave looks indicating ignorance. He glanced back at the wing entrance with a shudder.

Rowan lit his fourth consecutive cigarette with the burning end of the previous one and swiped the pile of ash with his shoe. The balcony scene was almost here.

Timothy said his final line. The lights went down, and Edward began his ascent up the ladder. Lisa waited until he reached the top, paused to give Walter a worried smile, and then climbed up. Grizz held off on any of the balcony lights until Lisa was safely positioned at the back. A pale light shined on Edward.

I know you fellas like the sun, but the truth is, it's nothing compared to the moon. If the sun had its way, we'd all burn. The moon is what keeps us spinning. It protects us from that fiery psychotic in the sky.

Maura sat in Lisa's chair, imagining herself doing the scene with Edward. Allison and Timothy stood far apart in the crossover.

Walter was watching Lisa from below. Rowan turned to the back of the theater, expecting to see Jenny. She was gone.

The chrysanthemums are for mom. The tulips are for Mrs. Perkins. But this, this single rose. This is for my love. This is for Agatha. Is someone there?

Rowan followed the pathway of the catwalk. Jenny had moved from the offices and was now standing next to Grizz at the edge. They looked to be in a heated discussion.

I said, is someone there?

The detective turned back to the stage just in time to see the light shine on Lisa Pluviam's half of the balcony. She toppled over the rail, plunging twenty feet and landing face first with a sharp, sickening crack of her neck.

5

WHAT HAPPENED?

8:07 p.m. Friday, April 5th

In the short-lived space between Lisa Pluviam landing on the stage and the piercing screams emanating from the audience, Rowan stood, frozen with consternation. The border between stage and auditorium shattered, the illusory sets reverting back to their cold artificiality when confronted with the repulsive reality of a corpse. Against all logic, and yet exactly as foretold, The Red Rising Theater had become the scene of a murder.

As Grizz signaled for the two grips to turn on all the lights, Jenny Pluviam's shoes rattled along the iron catwalk over the tumultuous sea of commotion from the audience. On the stage,

Rowan raised his hands, pleading for calm. The crowd, far past the point of reason, ignored his words, surging forward in a mindless collective. A few patrons dashed off down the hallway, trampling over Officer Young.

Walter couldn't see the ghastly scene in front of the tower, but he surmised what had happened and quickly gathered Timothy and Allison from the crossover. "Get to the dressing room." When they emerged from the wing, Maura was standing in the center with bleary eyes and a trembling jaw. The first ghostly echoes of screaming had told her what happened. Allison's voice cracked as she confirmed it. "Lisa fell from the balcony. I think she's dead."

Back in the auditorium, a single member of the crowd was allowed through to the stage. "I'm a doctor."

Rowan said, "Do not touch her. Leave her alone."

"She may still be alive."

Rowan looked down at the body. Thankfully, only a little of her face was exposed, but her neck now had three flabby folds of loose skin as if the bellows of an accordion were keeping the head attached. The limbs were twisted pathetically at impossible angles. One hand remained upright, the fingers bent and bloody with cracked scarlet nails, the other folded flush against the forearm. "She's evidence. Nothing more. Come on now." Jenny heaved herself up the corner of the stage. *Christ.* Making a mad dash, Rowan intercepted her path to the body, forcing her head onto his shoulder and whirling her around to keep the horrific image out of her sight. "Do not look. Do not look, Jenny."

She struggled against him, but all her strength had been sapped just getting near her dead sister. Her voice whimpered as her body melted in the detective's protective embrace. "Lisa, no."

As the tenor of the crowd toned down, individual comments became decipherable.

She just fell like a sack of potatoes.

For God's sake, cover her up. Give the woman some dignity.

That must be her sister. Horrible. Just horrible.

Walter called out from the hall. "Police are on their way."

Rowan caught sight of Young entombed within the crowd, a trickle of blood dripping from above his temple. "Good. Perhaps some real ones will show up."

Edward finally climbed down the ladder and took a step toward Rowan. A crunch underneath his shoe stopped him. One of Lisa's glass earrings had come loose and now lay shattered underneath his foot. "What happened?" he asked with quivering uncertainty.

With the shock finally worn down, Walter managed to get everyone's attention. "Ladies and gentlemen, please return to your seats. The police will be here soon to take a statement from each and every one of you. No one can leave yet."

They can't keep us here.

This is outrageous. We have rights.

A woman vomited in the middle of the aisle and the frenzy began all over again. Fights broke out among the whirlpool of bodies. Young disappeared into a melee of fists and elbows.

Rowan's eyes caught Edward's.

Edward asked once again, "What happened?"

In Lisa's office, Walter sifted through the desk while Rowan tried to talk sense to the man in charge. It was not Sergeant Grady, but rather his corporal, a burly fellow named O'Sullivan. His job was a simple one. He was to restore order and find out if any crime had been committed. The audience had been questioned and allowed to leave. The auditorium was now eerily quiet, save for some small cop chatter and the occasional crackling pop of a camera bulb. Order had been restored.

As for a crime, it appeared that not a single one had been committed. Rowan was good friends with Sergeant Grady, so leeway had been granted and the cast kept in the dressing room after questioning. However, there was only so much leeway to grant and the hour was getting late. "Something might come up in the autopsy, but for the time being, there is nothing here that would indicate a murder."

Rowan fidgeted with desperation as he paced. "What about the suspects? None of them have fingerprints on file. A trip to the station would be in order, yes?"

O'Sullivan spoke very slowly. "They aren't suspects. There's no murder, so they can't be considered suspects. I have no reason to have them fingerprinted."

"Even if they did nothing, we have to have their fingerprints to match against the possible prints of an outside agent."

The corporal snapped, a rising tide of exhausted anger in his voice. "Am I speaking Chink? Is there some reason you aren't hearing me? There is no murder. We aren't looking for an outside agent. We have an accident on our hands, nothing that requires further investigation. I took their statements. Everyone in the audience saw the same thing you did. She fell. We've got the measurements and the prints of the corpse. That's all we can do."

"You're going to let them go free?"

Walter pulled the bottom drawer from its housing. O'Sullivan yelled, "Hey you, enough. You have no right to search in there."

Rowan moved into O'Sullivan's line of sight, blocking Walter. "The blood work will reveal her cause of death. If you do not get the prints of those five people—"

Walter added, "And Jenny."

"—and Jenny, then the killer will simply walk away, skip town and move on. There will be no way to track him down. This moment is vital to the case."

"There's no killer. There's no case. Jesus!"

Rowan knew everything the corporal said was proper protocol, but he also knew that Lisa Pluviam *had* been murdered. She fell, yes, but the fall had been compelled...somehow. Most grating of all, Rowan had failed to protect her. His only thought now was the delivery of justice, if only for her memory. "Corporal O'Sullivan, was there anything unusual found in the theater?"

He let loose with a frustrated breath. "A thirty-eight under the light board."

"Grizz?"

"If you mean Mr. Thompson, yes. When questioned, he informed us that it was his gun. He keeps it there in case there are any problems with the patrons."

In case someone boos? "Was it registered?"

"No. As I am sure you know, handguns do not require registration."

"Oh yes, I'm aware. Just wondering, were there any bullets in the gun?"

"One. But that's neither here nor there. There was not a single report of a gunshot nor did we find any casings."

Rowan nodded. "Did Mr. Thompson tell you why Jenny approached him on the catwalk during the balcony scene?"

O'Sullivan pulled out his notebook. "Thompson was having trouble with the Pluviam woman's light. It wouldn't function. He panicked and called Jenny Pluviam over to report the situation. By the time she crossed the catwalk, he had managed to fix the problem. It was a false alarm. That's when the actress fell." He snapped the notebook shut. "Now, Mr. Manory, it's time to send those people home."

Walter stood up from behind the desk. "Corporal, I think you might want to take a look at this."

O'Sullivan looked at what Walter had found. He grumbled; the man hadn't had more than three hours' sleep since the bombing. "Fine. We'll take her in. Just her though."

"But, everyone needs to be interviewed about this, in case of

84

collusion," Rowan argued. "Surely you realize—"

"Five minutes each, right here in this office! That's it. No more. I don't care who you are or who you know."

"Who I am or *whom* I know." O'Sullivan looked like he was going to take a swing, so Rowan bowed his head. "Thank you. I will make sure to impress upon Sergeant Grady how cooperative you were. Please send Maura Lewis first."

Williams waited for O'Sullivan to slam the door. "You won't be able to learn anything in five minutes."

"All I need is a starting point."

"What happened, Manory? No one went up the ladder. No one—"

"That's correct, Williams. No one touched her. Someone killed her though. One of them."

Maura bobbed her leg up and down uncontrollably and kept reaching for gum that wasn't in her pocket. "Grizz says that we don't have to stay here. We can go any time we want unless you charge us with a crime. Is that true? If that's true, I want to leave now."

"Miss Lewis, this is as difficult for me as it is for you. We have all suffered quite a shock this evening."

Her forehead pushed down, hardening the look of her face. She whined when she spoke, her voice showing none of its characteristic sing-song lilt. "I've already talked about it though. I told the cop everything."

"I would appreciate just a few more moments of your time. For Lisa."

Maura folded her arms and looked off to the side.

What a brat. "There seems to be some confusion regarding your home state. Which is it, Ohio or Iowa?"

"Ohio."

"And the city?"

She licked her lips. Her neck craned back a bit. "Trenton."

Far too long to answer that question, Miss Lewis. "Trenton?"

"Yes."

"Trenton, Ohio?"

Maura finally looked at Rowan. "Yes."

He made a loud, popping cluck with his tongue. "Where do you live now?"

"I already told the policeman where I live."

"Could you say it again for our records?" The detective's voice retained its pleasant tone.

"I'm tired of answering the same questions. If you're going to ask me something, ask me something new."

Rowan folded his hands on the desk. "My questions have not been difficult and, at the risk of embarrassing you, I must say that you seem unduly nervous."

"Was that a question? I don't know if you just asked me a question or made a comment." Maura's breath grew shallow. "I don't like cops."

"Neither do I, but you don't see me being defensive."

"Am I a suspect?"

"At this early stage of the investigation, everyone is a suspect, even Williams."

Walter smiled at the girl. "We've had a few cases where I made the final list."

Rowan said, "Why did you come to the second city?"

Maura told them about leaving home and working for different theaters in small towns on the way to Chicago. "My plan was to become famous. That's funny, huh? I got a role, but it was in this play. My luck in a nutshell. Something good happens to me and then…" She pulled rogue strands of black hair over her face.

Poor you. At the very least your neck is still intact. "Do you have any family?"

She shook her head.

"No family?"

"When you shake your head, that's what it means. I'm done talking, Mr. Manory. If you want to arrest me, do it now. Otherwise, I'll flounce."

A nerve. "If you had to guess who killed her—"

"I thought she fell."

"If she was killed, who would do it?"

On the verge of tears, Maura said the name. "Allie."

Rowan spread out his hands, finally satisfied with one of her answers. "Now, that is interesting. Why do you think Allison would want Lisa dead?"

"Cause Timothy was hauling Lisa's ashes."

Rowan's face lost its smugness. He looked to Walter. "What does it mean—hauling ashes?"

"I've never heard it before. Miss Lewis, you mean…"

"They were screwing, all right? Do you understand that? Do you know what *screwing* means or do you need me to draw you a picture?"

Rowan said, "Not necessary. How did you find this out?"

"Every time they rehearsed the first scene, I'd have to wait in the crossover. Timothy would reach under the table and pinch her butt. He did it from the third week on, but this week, he didn't do it. I figured they broke it off."

"A playful pinch does not necessarily mean they were engaged in a sexual relationship."

"Do you pinch Walt's butt?"

Walter's forehead lifted. "We can't argue with that logic, boss."

"Did Allison know about the affair?" asked Rowan.

Maura shrugged. "I'm not a mind reader."

Rowan thought back to that moment in the dressing room. *She did recognize me.* "One last question, Miss Lewis. Have we met before?"

"I'm leaving now, detective."

Rowan beamed. "As you wish. We may contact you later for more information as the case moves forward. One of the officers will drive you home."

"I'll walk."

"At this hour?"

She left without answering.

Walter shut the door. "You charmed the shit out of her, Manory."

"Tell me, Williams, was Miss Lewis behaving herself backstage?"

"No, she was acting immature; got quite upset at Tim. The weirdest part was she missed a cue on purpose, just to tell me a joke. Granted, it was a funny joke, but still. Of course, she wasn't the only one with problems. Tim was off all night. Even Edward messed up a few times. I'm no theater critic, but this was not a good performance. Though I must say, Allison was spot on."

Rowan lit his cigarette. "As of this moment, I do not suspect any of you of a crime. I want to make that clear, Edward. We are not certain any crime has even been committed."

Edward looked confused. "I think it's obvious a crime has been committed."

Rowan's eyebrows arched. "You do?"

"I also think it's ridiculous to say that none of us are suspects. As much as I hate to admit it, we know the note came from one of us."

You do not sound like you hate to admit it. "Then I can drop the charade. We are in complete agreement."

Edward leaned forward. "And we know that whoever wrote the note killed her."

Rowan started to nod but aborted it midway. "It's possible."

"Possible?"

"Probable but not certain."

"So who wrote the note? This becomes the question."

"No, it becomes *one* question. I have others. Where do you live, Edward?"

"Fifty-five West Taylor with my aunt. It's her house. I'm her caregiver."

"How long have you lived with her?" asked Rowan.

Edward slumped his shoulders. "My whole life."

"Lisa mentioned that you had never done any acting before. Why start now? Why this play?"

"That's not completely true. I acted in high school and I quite enjoyed it. It's easy enough. Someone acts, you *react*. It's not math. As for why I auditioned for this play, I saw an advert at the Wong Li Laundromat. It looked like fun."

"Do you have a regular job?"

"I'm a delivery driver for Garfield hospital."

Rowan stubbed out his cigarette, pulled out a fresh paper and casually played with it. "What sort of things do you deliver?"

"All sorts. Bandages, pads, needles—"

"Drugs?"

"Sometimes."

"Anything poisonous?"

"I see some of the names on the bottles, but I'm not a doctor or a chemist. I don't know what they do, and it isn't my job to know."

"Right. Let's talk about the play. Did Lisa seem strange to you, right before the two of you went up the ladder?"

Edward struggled to answer. "I wish I could say something helpful. Lisa was the same as always, except maybe a little nervous. We were all dealing with an extra dose of nerves tonight."

"And when you saw her fall, was there anything odd you noticed?"

"No, it happened too quickly. By the time I turned around, she was..." He looked away. "She was on the way down."

"I only ask you because *I* noticed something."

"What?" asked Edward.

"She did not jump, nor was she pushed. She simply toppled. Her torso bent forward and the wooden rail caught her stomach, causing her legs to go straight into the air. It was as if she were in a trance and did not see the rail." Rowan ripped the paper and tossed it. "What about Allison? Williams tells me that she made a rather unexpected appearance in the crossover?"

"It *was* strange, I'll admit that. While we were waiting in the dressing room, I asked her about it."

"And?"

"She said she wanted to wish Lisa good luck."

Rowan gave a gradual smile. It started as a twinkle in the eye and ended with smug confidence. "Do you believe her, Edward? Does she often come out to wish actors luck in the crossover?"

"No, but I don't know why she would lie."

Rowan snapped his fingers and Walter set the notebook on the table. "Did you know that Timothy was hauling Lisa's ashes?"

"What?"

"You do not know the saying?"

"No. Do you mean Tim killed her?"

Rowan shook his head. "I will rephrase. Was it common knowledge among the cast that the two of them were engaged in a sexual relationship?"

Sitting in the dimly lit office, Edward saw the image again in his mind. It was a rainy March day. He had forgotten his wallet and ran back into the theater. They were in the wing. Timothy had Lisa by the hair, pushing her face into the wall, his hand roughly grabbing between her legs. The smile leered on her face, and a lock of black hair clung to the corner of her craven mouth as he called her filthy, unspeakable names.

"Edward!"

"Huh?"

"Did you know?"

Edward swallowed. "Allie couldn't do this. Not in a million years."

Rowan paid close attention to Edward's face. "And what if I told you that Allison was behind the threat?"

Edward's cheeks turned the color of chalk. "Was she?"

Timothy stared straight at the floor with his mouth ajar. His responses came out in a numb monotone.

A pile of cigarette butts lay at Rowan's feet. "Where are you from, Timothy?"

"Grew up in Adair."

"Adair? I do not think I am familiar."

"It's a nine-hour drive without traffic. 'Bout a river's meander to Iowa."

"How many plays have you done? Professionally?"

"This is the third." Timothy sniffled.

"And how did you meet Lisa Pluviam?"

"Met her the day of the audition. Allie and I done come in together. I wasn't expecting nothing, but I knew Allie'd get the role; she was perfect for it. Then Jenny said she wanted both of us. We were over the moon."

Rowan pretended to examine his nails. "How long were you and Lisa involved?"

Timothy looked up. "You...you know?"

"She informed me," Rowan said matter-of-factly.

"We agreed to keep it a secret." Timothy's muscular frame appeared weak, seeming to collapse in on itself. "A few weeks, I didn't count the days."

"Was it you or she that ended the affair?"

"We didn't really bust up. She said we needed to cool it down..." He lost his composure and his voice whimpered like a mew coming out of a lion. "...that we needed to cool it down for a while in case Allie found out. Cause...the play...I'm sorry." Rowan motioned to Walter for a handkerchief. Timothy blew his nose and wiped at the tears welling in his eyes. "We had to stop seeing each other until the play was done finished. We didn't split up. Not like that."

Walter tapped his pencil on the notebook. "Manory, that's interesting."

"Quite right, Williams."

Puzzled, Timothy looked from one detective to the other. "What's interesting?"

Rowan jabbed his cigarette out on the desk. *Here we go.* "Lisa informed us only yesterday that she had ended the affair."

"Lisa said that?" His red-rimmed eyes blinked.

"What were her exact words, Williams?"

Walter flipped to an empty page. "Things have gotten stale between us, especially between the sheets."

"Horseshit!" Timothy leapt from his chair. His hands slammed on the desk.

Rowan didn't move. "Easy. Calm down, son. These things happen to the best of us."

"You're plum lying?"

Rowan raised his voice, sensing weakness. "Did Allison know you were hauling Lisa's ashes?"

"What the hell does that mean?"

"Did Allison know of the affair?"

"I don't think so."

"But maybe?"

"No. I don't know. I...I can't tell anything with that woman."

"Allison would be furious, wouldn't she?"

"Allie knows I sleep around. It's not a big deal. She wouldn't kill Lisa. Not Allie."

Rowan pointed to the badge on Grizz's arm. "How long have you been a communist?"

Grizz flinched. His voice sputtered. "Why…You…CCUC is the local carpenters union. It ain't a political affiliation, and I think you know that."

Rowan laughed. "Well, you know."

"No, I don't know. Why don't you explain it to me, real slow like."

"Not all communists are carpenters, but most carpenters are communists. I believe it's a prerequisite for joining the union."

"Jesus was a carpenter. Was Jesus a communist?"

Rowan held up a thumb and index finger, spaced a quarter of an inch apart. "Just a little bit."

Grizz tilted his head away. "It ain't none of your business, but I think the people should share in the wealth."

"And the misery?"

Grizz looked around the office. "Where's Jenn?"

"Miss Pluviam was taken to the hospital as a precaution."

"Why am I being questioned by a private dick?"

"Mr. Thompson, I am working with the police and have been given their blessing; please leave the questioning to me. Why don't you take me through the lighting mishap." With halting apprehension, Grizz retraced the story he had told the police.

Rowan learned that he bought the gun after a particularly bad beating suffered many years earlier. Grizz didn't see Lisa fall from the balcony because he was speaking with Jenny.

Rowan followed the lines on Grizz's worn face. *Out of everyone, you seem the least emotional.* "Lisa told us you were good friends."

"When you work together on a play, you become like a little family. We were only about ten years apart, so if I was going to bond with anyone in the cast, I guess it makes sense it would be Leece."

"Did she tell you about the death threat before today?"

"No, she told me this morning in her office. She…" Grizz pursed his chapped lips.

"Go on."

"She was all wonky, said she wanted to cancel the play. I guess you could say this is all my fault."

"Why is that?"

"'Cause I'm the stupid son of a bitch who convinced her to go through with it." He turned up his nose. "The whole reason I did it was 'cause you were here. It was your job to keep her safe. Right? Also, like I told you this morning, I think Maura made the threat. I didn't think she'd go through with it, though."

Grizz's words stung Rowan. *It was my job to keep her safe.* "This morning you accused Maura and then Edward. You were about to give me another name."

"Any one of those punks coulda done it. Whoever did do it, I hope they get what's coming to them."

Rowan nodded. "So do I, Mr. Thompson. So do I."

"Are we done? Can I go?"

"Certainly, Mr. Thompson." Rowan waited until Grizz got to the door. "Oh, just one more thing." He reached into Lisa's desk drawer. "You forgot your Chesterfields."

Rowan ran his fingers over the paper. "Miss Miller, we chose to interview you last for a very good reason."

Allison nodded. "I figured as much."

He asked her about the incident in the crossover.

"I thought Lisa needed some encouragement. When I got there, she looked horrified. Maybe she thought I'd break her concentration."

Walter said, "I'm sorry, Miss Miller, but I saw her face clear as day. Lisa Pluviam was not horrified. The woman was surprised. All three of us were surprised. You weren't supposed to be there."

She didn't respond.

Rowan said, "What were you holding in your hand?"

"I didn't have anything in my hand."

Walter scratched his cheek. "I hate to keep interrupting you, but it certainly appeared as if you were holding something. Your hand was clenched."

"No." Her face reddened.

Rowan slid the note across the table. "Tell me, what would make you want to kill Lisa Pluviam?"

It was then that Allison confessed.

Grady thought he would invite Rowan to have a little chat with McKinley in regards to the postmortem. It was more than a professional courtesy. Two days had passed since opening night, and he knew his friend had to be suffering over in his quaint little office on Wabash.

Rowan agreed with a matter-of-factness borne from helplessness and, hands wrapped on his aching knees, sat in the back of the police car. He had drawn countless diagrams of the theater and replayed the fall over and over in his head. Perhaps an autopsy would provide him with concrete answers.

Lisa Pluviam's body lay in the shallow white porcelain tub, stark naked with unsightly blue bulges peppered over her collarbone and thighs. The hands had been flexed into their rightful position and the still-crooked fingers snapped back into reasonable places. The cartilage of the nose had receded deep into the broken nasal bone, forming a cruel snout. Her gray mouth looked like that of an old woman, crumpled and drifting inward. Large black stitches ran down her chest and stomach.

The pathologist, McKinley, had spread her organs in trays positioned next to the body. He used his forceps to point while he talked. "I've been top to bottom, Sergeant."

"And?"

"No poison."

Rowan folded his arms. "Nonsense."

McKinley furrowed his brow. "Hey tubby, there are no injection marks on the body. The skin is not unduly stained and there is no erosion inside the throat. The bladder is not distended. That rules out quite a few poisons already."

Rowan corrected him. "A few poisons, not quite a few."

McKinley poked his tongue against his cheek. "The esophagus shows no softening. No perforations inside the stomach." He casually flipped her liver. "The liver has not yellowed. The upper respiratory tract is clean." He picked up the tray of kidneys and shook it. "These are perfect. The lungs are not congested. Heart's fine."

Rowan said, "What of the blood?"

"That's what I mean. We took a sample directly from the heart. This woman was not poisoned."

"You found nothing at all?"

McKinley shrugged. "There was some swelling in the brain, but it's perfectly justifiable, considering the impact."

Grady said, "So, she died of a broken neck?"

"C1 and C2 fractures. The way she must have landed, I'm surprised her head stayed on. Last week, we got a jumper over on the north side. This guy's head—"

"So, broken neck?"

"Well...yes."

The sergeant looked at Rowan. "Satisfied?"

Rowan muttered obscenities under his breath as he left the room. *How was she murdered?*

Grady caught up with him. "We released Allison Miller today. I held her as long as we could."

Rowan continued walking at a steady pace as he spoke. "I knew it would amount to nothing. Allison was fiercely jealous of Lisa's relationship with her boyfriend. The night before the play, Allison put the letter in her office. At the time, she had no idea Lisa had already received a threat."

Grady jogged by his side. "We can call it all an amazing coincidence now, right?"

Rowan whipped around, jabbing an angry index finger into Grady's chest. "Someone killed Lisa Pluviam in that theater. That someone is not going to get away with it."

He spread out his arms. "How? How do you make someone fall off a balcony?"

"I am going to find out. And where were you, Grady? I had to fight with your monkey, O'Sullivan, just to get five minutes with them."

"I woulda done the same thing he did. You heard McKinley. There's no murder." Grady pulled out a cigar and stuck it in the corner of his mouth. "I haven't seen the note. What did the Miller woman write anyway?"

"Something to the effect of, *If you don't stay away from Timothy, I'll kill you.* She even signed her name at the bottom. It is hard enough to believe a murderer makes a death threat, impossible to believe she would sign it. Allison Miller did not plan a murder, certainly not one this cunning and perfectly executed."

Grady shook his head. "The dame signed it? Christ, women make such awful criminals. Too much damn sincerity."

"That is not true at all. They often commit quite clever and devious crimes. Have you forgotten Alice Mayburg, who fed her husband to his own dogs? Ursela Randrovich. She stabbed herself three times to hide her murder. That took commitment. If only she had considered the angles of the blade. Irene Roberts committed the most brilliant murders I've ever come across. She almost—"

"It was a fucking joke, Manory."

Rowan stuttered. "Oh...yes, I...I see now."

"You're too wound up." Grady put his arm on Rowan's shoulder and walked him toward the door. "I'll wrap it up and you can forget all about it. Not every death requires a solution. No one touched her, no one poisoned her. Unless I type God on the report, we have no murderer. I'll send someone to meet you out front and drive you back. I'm sorry about this, Manory. I can tell you had a hard-on for the lady."

"Grady?"

"Yeah?"

"You told me at The Brown Bear that her name was familiar to you. Did you ever recall why?"

"Matter of fact, I did. Lisa Pluviam was a suspect in a murder case."

"When?"

"Back in 1912. Her boyfriend at the time, Clarence Williams, was found dead. Drowned."

"If the man drowned, why was murder suspected?"

"He drove from Chicago to Devil's Lake, Wisconsin to go skinny dipping in the middle of the night. Funny thing for a guy to do when he can't swim. His car was found abandoned in northern Illinois."

"How long was Lisa considered a suspect?" asked Rowan.

"About a day," said Grady, lighting his cigar and puffing it to life. "There's a town just south of the lake called Baraboo. According to the report, Clarence stopped off at a general store in the town to purchase some cigarettes. A witness, the owner's wife, saw a woman in his car. The police drove Lisa up to Baraboo to see if the wife could finger her."

"But she could not?"

"Nope. The witness said she wasn't the woman in the car. The department wasn't great at keeping records back then. There's only a one-sheet report in our files, but it has a bit of the witness's statement. She said the woman in Clarence's car was a fat blonde with a cigarette stuck in her mouth."

Rowan stopped just before the door. "Could you get me the name and address of the witness?"

Grady winced. "Dammit, Manory."

"Perhaps nothing will come of it, but it will do wonders for my peace of mind."

Just as Rowan suspected, the first elusive puzzle piece was falling into place.

6

SIX OR ZERO

1:23 p.m. Monday, April 8th

Walter leaned against the fractured black lacquer of the Brown Bear's bar. "Dave. Dave."

Dave Bowen was flipping through Grady's flyers, trying to find the least upsetting pictures to adorn his wall. "I can hear you just fine, Walter. You need another?"

"No, I need two anothers. Manory's drinking too."

"Yeah, he's drinking a lot more than he usually does." Over Walter's shoulder, the bartender could see his favorite customer perched in his usual spot at the center of the bar, scribbling furiously on a napkin. "Manory was drinking in the afternoon with

103

Grady last week. You might want to keep an eye on the guy. It's only Monday for Christ's sake."

Walter shrugged. "He's a little depressed."

"He's always depressed. The cheese fell off that guy's cracker a long time ago. Tough case?"

"Oh, the worst, Dave. It's the worst."

Dave propped a forearm onto the bar. "What happened?"

"We were hired to protect a woman. She got killed."

"Well done. Now I know who not to hire. Any suspects?"

Walter bent his head. "Six. Or zero. I don't know. It's complicated."

"How was she killed?"

"She fell."

"Someone pushed her?"

"Not exactly."

"She trip?"

"No. She just..." Walter held up his hand and let it drop onto the bar with an ugly splat. "...fell."

"It don't sound like much of a mystery. People fall all the time. I fell in the doorway today. No investigation was necessary."

"Yeah, but no. This woman was definitely murdered. She received a death threat before it happened."

"A-ha. Now I understand." Dave polished a glass. "Don't it stand to reason that the person who made the threat is the one who killed her?"

"You'd think so, wouldn't you?" said Walter.

"Maybe someone will confess. Guilty conscience."

"Someone did confess."

Dave spread his arms out wide. "Case closed then."

"No. The woman who confessed didn't kill her. Or maybe she did, but we can't be sure."

"Why's that?"

Walter let out a frustrated breath. "Because the victim got a separate death threat."

"Two death threats?" Dave sighed. "Doesn't sound like a very popular woman."

"I know, right?"

"But you said someone confessed?"

"No, she didn't confess to killing her. She only confessed to sending her one of the death threats. We have to find out who sent the other one."

"I see." Dave leaned over on the bar with his head resting on both palms. "Maybe I'm stupid—"

"A distinct possibility."

"—but doesn't it sound like she wasn't murdered. If this person who threatened her—"

"Allison."

"If Allison didn't kill her, then wouldn't it be possible that the other person who threatened her didn't kill her either? I mean, why put stock in one threat if you're not gonna put stock in the other? You said yourself she fell. What am I not getting?"

Walter tried to put the reason together in his head. "Yeah,

but....You don't...I told you it was complicated. It's even more complicated when I say it out loud."

"I'm just trying to help."

Walter feigned offense. "Hey. Hey! I can't discuss the case with you. This is official detective business. You know what, give me *two* beers and *two* gin and tonics. That way I won't be tempted to come back and reveal anything more."

A shrill, pitiless voice came from the back room. "David! It's time for your shot."

Dave's stomach tightened before he realized his wife was right. Just the sound of her voice caused a painful cramp to overtake his body. He loved the woman, he just didn't want her to say anything to him. "Thank you, sweetie." He reached under the bar, pulling out a wooden box and a black rubber tube.

Walter stood on his toes to get a look. A neat row of syringes lined along the box's edge with a bottle of clear liquid squat in the center. He watched in fascination as Dave wrapped the tube around his arm and drew the liquid into a needle. "Is that for the syph?"

"No, dummy. I'm diabetic. It's insulin"

"Don't you have to go to a hospital for that stuff?"

Dave looked at him and smiled.

Walter gave a slow nod with a cracked grin. "You don't ask me anything more about the case, and I won't say anything about the personal pharmacy you got back here." He negotiated his way around a line of fake palm trees and then maneuvered the four drinks onto Rowan's table. "I think Dave just solved the case. For a bartender, that guy's really smart. What are you writing?"

Rowan dropped his pen on the table. "It's nothing."

Walter rotated the napkin.

1912–Clarence Williams murdered

19??–Pluviam sisters move to New York

1933–They return to Chicago

Timothy Edward Allison Maura–born 1912ish

Grizz–What is Lisa's connection to Grizz?

"Still on that, huh?"

"We need a motive."

"Revenge for the murder of this Clarence Williams character twenty years ago? That's the motive?"

"Lisa told us she had no skeletons in her past. We now know this to be false. At least it is something to go on. In any event, it is better than what I had been considering."

"Let me tell you Dave's idea 'cause it really got me to thinking."

Rowan's eyelids drooped. "God help us."

"Imagine this. All those years ago, Clarence Williams…Hey, he had my name. Williams *is* a popular name. Anyway, Clarence got drunk and pulled a brodie. He went into the water and drowned. No murder. And Lisa just lost her balance and fell. Now we're in a bar agonizing over two perfectly reasonable deaths."

Rowan burped. "Et tu, Williams?"

"How was she killed?"

"If I hear that question one more goddamn time."

"We have to answer it, don't we? Do you have any ideas?"

Rowan didn't. He only had contempt for doubt. This murder, this elegant, perfect murder only seemed not to exist.

Walter drank half his beer in one swig. "No one thinks it was foul play but us, and I have to be honest with you, my faith isn't the strongest."

"When we learn why she was killed, we will discover how she was killed."

Walter pulled back from the table. "You've told me the exact opposite before."

"Poppycock." Rowan burped again.

"I'm sure of it. You used to say if we knew how it was done, we would learn why. I remember, clearly."

"That's because you don't listen. At the moment, we have six suspects. Way too many. Three would be a far more manageable number."

"Agreed. Let's knock it down. Filius seems honest."

Rowan cackled. "Edward says the right things. The killer always says the right things because he knows the right things to say. Edward works for a hospital, which means he may have access to poisons."

"Lisa wasn't poisoned."

"He was the closest to her at the time."

"You mean he was the closest one to do nothing. No one touched her. Let's focus on what we know. Lisa got two threats. We know Allison wrote one of them."

Rowan stared off into the distance, stroking his stubbly chin. "What is more interesting is that Lisa did not tell us about the second note. Think about that. She receives the first threat and immediately comes to see me, a perfectly rational response. Then, the day we come to protect her, she finds Allison's threat in her office—the very office where she had found the previous one. What does she do? Nothing. She stuffs it in a bottom drawer without a second thought. Does not even bother to mention it to us. Why? Because she knew it to be cock and bull the moment she read it."

"So, we cross Allison off the list."

"Not until we find out what she was up to in the crossover. However, the others interest me more. Timothy comes to mind."

"Passion, unrequited love, he's a solid suspect. I mean, besides the total lack of evidence."

"I must find out from Jenny what Lisa thought of her relationship with Timothy. Was he delusional? Was he not ready to give up the affair?"

"Speaking of Jenny Pluviam. Blonde hair, smoker, pleasantly plump...filthy, filthy mouth."

"It fits perfectly. Why would she kill Clarence? Because of jealousy. Why would she wait twenty-three years to murder her sister? The inheritance."

"I'm a sucker for filthy broads. Just imagine the thoughts going through her mind."

"Williams."

"Sorry. What?"

"I will go to see Jenny tomorrow to offer my official condolences along with some carefully worded questions."

"What do you make of Grizz?"

"The gun staged under the light board was not for protection nor was the problem with the light genuine. Indeed, our communist friend troubles me—especially now that Grizz is a wanted man."

"Wanted for what?"

"You should read the paper. Our man Grizz was seen at the Federal Building before it exploded. His picture is everywhere."

Walter held up the napkin. "What's this about the connection between Lisa and Grizz?"

Rowan sneered, his fat cheeks smashing his eyes into slits. "Suicide."

Walter nearly choked on his beer.

"I do not like it either, but everything must be considered. Lisa was not poisoned and there was no physical injury before the fall. What are we left with? Electricity, hypnosis, a strong wind? Reasonable explanations are thinning fast. If there was some ideological connection between them, then perhaps she would have killed herself for the cause. It's nonsense, mind you. I cannot conceive a way in which her death would be beneficial to Grizz.

Yet, I know there was something between them. He was smoking in her office."

"They were friends? Maybe she let him smoke there."

"I remember Lisa disdainfully waving at the smoke from my cigarette. I get the feeling it was Grizz's prerogative to do exactly as he wished when he was in her presence."

"We've forgotten Maura."

"Oh, my friend, I have not forgotten. Maura Lewis. From Trenton. Thirty-six out of the forty-eight states have a Trenton."

"Clever girl."

"Foolish girl. Every state has a Washington. Lie only when the research has been done. Alas, Trenton, Ohio exists. This will be one of your jobs tomorrow. Do you know anyone in eastern Ohio?"

Walter nodded smugly. "I have people everywhere. I don't burn bridges the way you do. If there's a Maura Lewis from Trenton, I'll find her."

"Good. Also, check the respective residences of the cast. If they are not at home, feel free to snoop around and talk with a landlord or neighbor. If any doors happen to be loose..."

"Do you think Jenny will talk to you?"

"I do not know. Perhaps she blames me. Perhaps she is right."

"The day after her sister's funeral. She won't be in the best mood."

"That will make two of us."

Walter rolled his head around until something or other cracked in his neck. "By the by, when are we going to get out of this city?"

"We are in the middle of the most inexplicable and complicated case of our career. Is this the appropriate time to discuss our future?"

"You must have given some thought to retirement. Don't you want to go somewhere more conducive to…not murder?"

"Chicago is the only place I have ever called home, Williams. I do not live here because I enjoy it, but rather, because it is where I belong."

Walter leaned over the table, his fob clacking against the wood. "Now you're just being stubborn."

Rowan licked a paper and rolled it sloppily between his brown fingertips. "Then I am stubborn. I have no problem admitting it. At my age, change is more frightening than death."

"Look at you—can barely roll your cigarette. What's really painful is watching you eat. The fork shakes when you hold it. I'm scared you're going to stab yourself."

"My brain is just as fast as it ever was."

"Oh, yeah? Then how come…" Walter clapped his mouth shut.

Rowan scowled. "Go ahead. Say it, Williams. How come I took this case? You think me a fool."

Walter stared at the table. "Now is the time, boss. The average man lives to be about fifty-eight."

"I am well aware of my impending demise."

"Do you really want to spend your remaining years in

Chicago? I know I don't. I'm tired of living in the most dangerous city in America. If the people don't kill you, the cold or the heat will finish the job."

"Maybe, I do not want to spend my last eleven years with you. Perhaps being murdered would be preferable. Have you considered the possibility?"

"We could move to Los Angeles in a year's time. Hell, we could move there next month. I was talking with my friend, Bill Davies. He lives out there."

Rowan giggled. "The one who shot himself?"

Walter protested. "His gun went off accidently. Bill pulls in six-hundred a month, double that before the banks went under."

"Highway robbery. Mr. Davies should be paying the clients, not the other way round."

"Not the point. His cases? Love affairs. That's it. Wives hire him to follow their husbands to motels or back alleys or wherever. Occasionally, he gets hired to look into some sabotaged crops. Nothing heavy. No stabbings, no shootings, no poisonings, no…fallings. In a few years, you can retire. I'll find my own Watson to boss around. You'll only have to see me for one of these drunken bullshot sessions on the weekends. It's the smart move."

Rowan rubbed his hands through scarce strands of hair.

"Think about it."

"Fine, Jesus. After we solve this murder, I will go with you to Los Angeles."

Walter's eyes widened. "Seriously? This isn't just drunk talk?"

"This is completely drunk talk." Rowan lifted his glass and held it up to the dusty sunlight. "Williams, what did you bring me?"

Walter put the glass under his nose. "It's gin."

"I have been drinking scotch all afternoon."

"And I got you two gins?"

"Apparently so."

"Dave! Dave!"

The bartender laid down a stack of acceptable flyers and jogged to the table. "What's the rumpus, boys?"

Rowan pointed at Maura's name on the napkin. "Dave, do you know what it means to haul someone's ashes?"

"Yeah, it means to bump uglies."

"How did you know that?"

"My nephew says it."

"Is your nephew from Ohio?"

"Naw, he's from the neighborhood. Is this what you guys called me over for? I got a stack of flyers, and I have to slap more on the wall before Grady comes back."

Walter's body jerked to life. He grabbed Rowan's arm. "Dave, ask Manory if you should slap more on."

"Why would I do that?"

"Just ask him." He grinned from ear to ear.

"But—"

"Goddamnit, Dave. Do this one thing for me. Ask Manory if you should slap more on. Do it now. Now!"

"Manory, should I slap more on?"

Rowan's face grew serious, smoldering edges forming at the corners of his lips. "Williams is not a moron. And no, you shouldn't slap him."

Walter slammed his hand on the table. "Zing!"

The chandelier's reflection wavered on the restaurant's red-and-white checkerboard floor, surrounding Edward and Maura in an octagonal prison of light. The air-conditioning unit banged to life, then droned an otherworldly hum, dying after a few minutes before starting the tortuous process all over again.

"Do you think she was murdered, Eddie?"

Edward held a tongue sandwich in front of his mouth. "She didn't just happen to fall off that balcony the same day the note said she would die. The odds are astronomical."

"Maybe she was hypnotized." Maura grew determined when he laughed at the suggestion. "What? I've seen it."

"You believe in that nonsense?"

"Damn right I do. My mom took me to see the Great Renaldo a long time ago. He brought a woman on stage, sat her in a chair—this broad was clean-cut too; she looked like a dentist or a professor, something genuine, you know. She wasn't trash, that's the point I'm making. Anywho, he took out his pocket watch—"

"He waved it in the air?"

"Yes!"

"Then he told her she was getting sleepy?"

"You've seen his show?"

"What was the punch line?"

As Maura removed the pickles from her sweitzer cheese sandwich, piling them neatly on one side of the plate, she described the tense atmosphere of the tent, the woman taking off her shoes and peeling a banana with her feet, and the gasps of the audience as she dangled near the top of the pole.

Edward took a bite. "Mmm-hmm. A plant."

"Huh?"

"He paid her. She was instructed."

"How did she peel a banana with her feet without being hypnotized? Answer me that, Sherlock."

"Probably worked in the circus, some kind of gorilla act or something." Edward winced.

Maura nodded at his sandwich. "It's disgusting, isn't it? Just thinking about you putting that in your mouth makes me want to toss my cookies. A cow used it to taste food, and now you're tasting the thing the cow tasted with. It's perverted."

Edward shook his head. "Meat's good, there's just too much mustard. It's healthy, lots of iron." He held it toward her. "Try it."

"Are you trying to slip me some tongue?"

"Now that's funny. That's a keeper."

With a sly, slow blink she seemed to tell him that she already knew. "My one-woman act is coming soon. I'm gonna knock 'em dead." Her hand dug through her purse. "Forgot my notebook. Remind me of that line later so I can write it down."

Edward returned to the subject of murder. "I don't think we can go with hypnosis. I'm sure the solution is simple, something we've seen before. That's the way it is in detective novels. The killer is right in front of your face; you meet him in the first chapter."

"They arrested Allie. She could—"

"Allie's free."

"What?" Maura's jaw dropped.

Edward wiped a dab of mustard from his chin. "The cops let her go. I went to see her last night. Wanted to cheer her up."

"And?"

"She's inconsolable. Timothy hasn't been home since the cops released her. Allie has no idea where he is."

"Gossip, Edward. I want gossip."

"I'll tell you everything I know. First off, Allie was aware of Tim's infidelity. They had a...I don't know what you'd call it—a license to engage in—"

"He could plow any field he wanted?"

"Basically. Allie could ignore it as long as she was shielded from the details. But then came this play, and she had to go to work with the details, so she began to resent him. The weekend before opening night, Tim and Lisa went to his dad's farm together. It's some little country town."

"Adair."

Edward shrugged. "Maybe."

"Tim told me it was called Adair."

"Whatever. When Tim got back, he told Allie it was over between him and Lisa. She was ecstatic. It wasn't so apparent to me just how much she loved him."

Maura harrumphed. "Girls are so dumb."

"Thursday night, she went through Tim's wallet while he was in the bath."

"She found a love letter?"

"No."

Maura looked around the restaurant, seeming to search for the answer and waxing quite enthusiastic with several guesses.

Waving them all aside, Edward said, "Allie found an Eisenberg business card."

Maura slumped in her chair. "Oh."

"He's good friends with the people who work there. He got me a good deal on some earrings for my aunt."

"Those were so cute. I need some earrings. Jade looks good against my skin."

"Listen. I don't know if you've ever seen the Eisenberg logo, but it's a big diamond ring. That logo is right on the front of the card. When Allie saw it, she got it in her head that Tim was ring shopping, and she knew he wasn't doing it for her. After Tim fell asleep, she wrote Lisa a threatening letter. Allie took it to the theater that very night and put it on her desk." Edward stopped talking long enough for the waiter to set two coffees on the table and then continued with a hushed, conspiratorial tone. "My theory, and mind you it's just that—a theory—is that Tim proposed to Lisa during their weekend and she turned him down. Maybe he bought her a ring and maybe he didn't, but I think Allie may have been on the right track."

She gasped. "And Tim killed Lisa because she broke up with him. Wait, no. No, that doesn't make sense."

"Why not?"

"Because when we all learned about the death threat, Tim said we should cancel the play. He was the first one to speak."

"Of course he was. Once he found out a detective was there and the police were involved, he panicked. Whatever his plan was, he'd be discovered. Allie's note was the only thing that saved him. It was a convenient distraction. Now she's free and he's nowhere to be found. Why would he run if he's innocent?"

Maura shuddered. "We've been spending every day with a murderer. And he's still out there somewhere."

"Don't quote me. I'm not married to the idea. It could have been someone else."

"That's even worse, an unknown murderer, still on the loose. It could be Jenny or Grizz or…" She grew quiet, daring not to say it.

"Or me? Is that what you were going to say? Maura, if you think I'm capable of murder, I don't know what to tell you."

"Then, I'll ask you, and that'll be the end of it. Did you write the death threat?"

Edward put down the sandwich. "No, I didn't. And that's the truth."

"Aces. Now ask me."

"Ask you what?"

"Ask me if I wrote the note."

"I already know you didn't. You're a good person."

Maura rolled her eyes, but a flutter came to her chest all the same. "It was nice of you to see Allie. Hopefully she makes it to the shindig." She tapped a finger on the rim of his coffee cup. "How can you drink it black?"

"Are you going to criticize everything I eat and drink? I don't like milk."

"What's wrong with you? Everybody likes milk. It's best during the winter."

"Why is that?" asked Edward.

"When it gets delivered, you let it sit out for a while so's it freezes." Maura demonstrated with her hands. "The cream separates and rises to the top, the lid pops off, and you spoon out the frozen cream and melt chocolate all over it. I'm shaking just thinking about how good it is."

"You have milk delivered?"

"I used to. Acksherly, it's been a while, but I remember doing that all the time when I was a kid. My mom wanted to strangle me."

Edward grabbed hold of Maura's shoulders, squaring her body to his. "Look at me. Now say it. Ack."

"*Ack.*"

"Choo."

"*Choo.*"

"Uhhh."

"*Uhhh.*"

"Lee."

"*Lee.*"

"Actually."

"*Acksherly.*"

"Close enough."

Maura snuck a peek at the bill. "Jeez Louise, the coffee's expensive here."

Edward pulled out his wallet. "I figured I would get it."

"Yeah, I know, but still."

With the arrival of early evening, they settled on a park bench, away from the thick patches of mosquitoes darting through the air. Maura stared at the low, golden sun slowly disappearing from the sky. "This reminds me of the times I'd hide up on my roof back home and watch the sunset. My mom would run around the house searching for me. Hey, do you think Jenny will pay us anything for the rehearsal time?"

"Probably not. The agreement was for actual shows. I'm sure Jenn lost a lot of money on it."

"Great. That's just swell. More good luck." She put her hand on his. "I was counting on that money. At least you got nothing to worry about, what with the delivery gig at the hospital."

"I quit."

"Why would you do a thing like that?"

His fingers slipped between hers. "It might sound silly, but I think I want to give acting a real shot. This play didn't end well, obviously, but I've had more fun during the last six weeks than I've ever had. Of course, a lot of that was thanks to you. I wish we'd had some scenes together."

Maura twisted around, propping her knees onto the bench. "Eddie, I've got a proposition for you. If you say no, it's okay, really. With the play kaput, I can't afford to stay where I'm at. Acksherly, I'm gonna get kicked out from my place any day now. How about I stay at your house, just for a little while? It won't be a freeloader situation. I can cook…well, strike that, I don't know how to cook. But I can clean and take care of Christine. Just until I figure out what I'm gonna do. I'll stay out of your hair."

Edward grew excited. "That'll be perfect. We could go on auditions together. When we get cast, we'll help each other out with our lines."

When his hand fell on her bare knee, Maura, in an effortless, uncharacteristically graceful motion, grabbed the sides of Edward's head and kissed him. Edward tensed for a moment then eased into her lips. When they finally separated, he stared, awestruck by her courage.

Maura gave him an adorable, innocent smile with thin, wet lips. "You weren't going to do it, so I had to."

7

THE DIRECTOR

10:09 a.m. Tuesday, April 9th

Large areas of field and forest separated the stately houses along
the North Shore sidewalk. The neighborhood seemed lovely to
Rowan at first, with its splendid seclusion and absence of prying
eyes. *An ideal place to be alone with one's thoughts.* As he neared
the Pluviam residence, however, the opportunity for unobservable
murder occurred to him. The thought extrapolated in his mind so
paranoiacally that, when he finally made a turn at Minnifield,
Rowan half expected to find Jenny dead on the sidewalk, her neck
grotesquely mirroring her sister's.

He passed a small group of Oaks and came upon a picket

fence with an open gate. Two garbage cans lay toppled over at the curb, empty bottles of peroxide rolling back and forth across the middle of the street and a potato chip bag flitting in the hot breeze. He set the cans upright and rather thoughtlessly sifted through the layers of trash. Lisa's silver dress lay crumpled at the bottom, brown blood stains dried into the collar. An unnatural sound, rather like a stick snapping under an anxious foot, came from the trees behind him. Rowan saw no one standing there when he whirled around. *Stop scaring yourself, old man.*

The doubling of items in Jenny's living room gave clear evidence two people had lived there. There were exactly two sofas, two chairs, two coffee tables, two rows of bookshelves, two grandfather clocks, and most unusual of all, two framed pictures of the Christ.

Jenny appeared well-recovered from the traumatic shock of Friday night, a bit morose, but calm. It was as if she were on guard against any unnecessary histrionics. She brought Rowan some tea in the living room. It took her two trips.

He laid the saucer on the coffee table and pinched the teacup's delicate handle. "I wish to offer my deepest apologies for not attending the funeral. I was horribly detained."

She leaned one half of her body onto the chair, forearm against the arm rest, and then settled the other side before she spoke. "It doesn't matter, no one else came either. It was for the best. Lisa looked like a pig drenched from a river, all bloated and fleshy. I suppose I shouldn't judge. Dead isn't a good look for anybody."

"I noticed her dress in the garbage. It must have brought back some painful memories."

"It doesn't fit me." She winked at him. "The police brought her stuff here last night. Didn't want it—though I did hang on to the shoes. We had the same sized feet. I can still use the shoes."

"Lisa told me you lived together all your lives. It will be strange for you now. A person gets used to things."

Jenny picked a tuft of lint off her shirt. "I was prepared. I think Lisa was moving on to bigger and better productions than my little play. She got great notices from *The Farmer's Daughter*. Such a trifling bit of sentimentality. Were you unfortunate enough to see it?"

"Yes, I was. How did the two of you become interested in theater?"

"I think we were inspired by our Uncle Alan, the vagabond of the family, always borrowing money. He was in a traveling comedy troupe, and he would regale us with his tales of the stage. Alan was the only one we wanted to talk to at holiday gatherings. There's always one fun relative." Jenny pointed to the books on the mantel. "Our senior year we took drama together. I wasn't very good onstage, but I liked to write."

"And Lisa liked to act?"

"A born performer. She had to have someone clap every time she smiled. Lisa could start up a conversation with anyone about anything. Even if she knew nothing about the topic, she could fake it. The exact opposite of me. I wasn't a very popular girl in high school."

"No? That is difficult to imagine."

She cachinnated. "My God, you actually made me laugh. Here I thought you were a complete drip."

Rowan walked to the mantel for a closer look at the books. "I see you went to Saint Martin's High School?"

Jenny nodded. "We graduated the same year."

Rowan raised an eyebrow. "You were twins?"

"No, our mother was crazy. When Lisa finished the eighth grade, Mom made her repeat it, just so we would graduate together. Leece hated me for a long time for that."

"A bit eccentric, but not unreasonable."

"We had two of the same toy and two of every article of clothing. Our entire childhood was unreasonable."

"And after graduation?"

"We got jobs at Hull House."

Rowan was impressed. "Straight out of high school? My goodness."

Jenny shook her head. "This was back when it was nothing but a barn. You had to wipe shit off your shoes before you went in. Lisa sewed costumes, and I made a lot of coffee. For payment, we got to see the shows for free. Daddy wasn't too happy with us, said we were wasting our lives."

"Why did you end up going to New York?"

"Because Daddy was right. Lisa got some bit roles, usually looking pretty and giving a few lines of exposition. I was writing, but I never got credit. We were both getting older. It was time to shit or get off the pot."

"What do you mean, you did not get credit?"

"Have you ever seen a production of *The Mill*?"

"Yes. Nigel Larsen."

Jenny frowned, her voice soaked with contempt. "Nigel Larsen needed help writing his name in the snow. And you could do it with tweezers."

"But—"

"Lots of women write plays, Mr. Manory. But their names don't make it on the playbill for one reason or another. There's always some lowlife willing to take credit. That's why we're called script girls."

"I see." *I would be just as bitter.*

"Lisa met a playwright named Abe Freeman. He was an older gentleman, a real warhorse. He had been a professor at the Playhouse in New York. He wrote us letters of recommendation and, somehow, we were accepted sight unseen. I think Lisa spent a night or two in his bed, but she never admitted it. That's the only way I could imagine Abe doing something like that for us." Jenny grinned. "Leece was always ready to go the extra mile."

"When was this?" asked Rowan, picturing the timeline in his head.

"About nineteen…thirteen."

One year after Clarence Williams was murdered. "Did you have your accident while you were in school?"

Jenny looked at Rowan from the corners of her eyes. "Before. It happened on my second day in New York." A harsh squint came to her face as she told the story. "It was a few days before Christmas so the streets were crowded. We were walking along the curb, and I remember having this terrible fear that I was going to slip and land on my ankle and break my foot off. There was no snow, but the ground was covered with thin ice. Lisa could see I was off balance and...and the bitch pushed me. How funny is that? I fell into the street. The car swerved but not enough. Before I knew it, there was a goddamn tire on my hand." She looked at her stump. "All the bones were crushed. The only thing I could feel was hot blood on my wrist. Smelled like copper."

"Yes, it does."

"I screamed and screamed, but nobody helped. They paused to look, but then they just went on walking. Lisa just stood there, gawking." Jenny's mouth twisted. "I passed out and when I woke up, I had this beauty." She pulled out a Beechnut with her teeth. Rowan bent down to light it. "It's nice to be able to smoke in the living room without Lisa throwing a fit."

Funny, Grizz could smoke in your sister's office with no problem. "Your accident did not deter you from your studies though?"

"Lisa and I hadn't started yet. We called the school and took an extended break. I learned to type one-handed and began my studies the next year. I'm a very determined woman, Mr. Manory."

"By my estimation you spent twenty years in New York. What

were you doing?" Rowan's tone became businesslike, flat and demanding.

"After graduation, we taught. When Daddy died, we figured, why not come back and give Chicago another shot? Everyone we knew was gone or dead."

"Which hospital performed the amputation?"

"I don't remember the name. It was a long time ago." A refuse truck shuddered to a halt on the street outside, followed by the angry beep of a motorist. Jenny stomped to the window and closed it with a bang. "Now, detective, I've answered your questions patiently, probably questions you had already asked Lisa. What are you doing here? What is this?"

"When we were in your office Friday morning, you told me you thought the death threat was faked. Do you still believe that? Even now?"

No answer.

"I am going to apprehend your sister's killer."

She exhaled a long puff of smoke onto the smoldering tip of the cigarette, making it glow. Her foot tapped several times against the floor. "All right. Let's assume she was killed. Who did it? Why? How?"

"Who is Grizz?" said Rowan with no intention of letting Jenny derail his questioning.

"Grizzy was a friend of Lisa's. She's the one who introduced us. He's a member of the carpenters union, and I needed someone who could build the tower. I don't know much about him. We never chit chatted about anything personal."

"When he called you over to the catwalk, before Lisa fell, what did he say to you?"

Jenny looked down. It reminded Rowan of Lisa staring at the floor in his office. "I saw Grizz motion for me to come over. When I got there, he told me there was a problem with Lisa's light."

"But there was no problem, was there?"

"No, there wasn't. I told him to try it again, and it worked just fine. Grizzy's about as sharp as a marble."

"Did he reach under the light board?"

"Yes, he did. Just before—"

"Did you know he had a gun under the light board?"

Jenny's face went blank.

Rowan said. "Why would he have a gun there?"

"He shouldn't have."

"I thought so too. It seemed a strange place for a weapon. Whom would he shoot from the catwalk?" Rowan dragged from his cigarette as he paced. "How did the casting process go?"

Jenny remained still, turning her head to follow Rowan. "We put out an ad in the Tribune and at some of the local businesses. I wanted a young cast. Experience wasn't what I was looking for. Timothy and Allison were the first ones I chose. Allie was perfect for Stella because she has an endless supply of self-doubt. I cast Timothy because he's dumb and masculine. I knew Lisa would like him."

"Did you know how much she would like him?"

"I kept my nose out of it."

"But you knew?"

"What Lisa did with her box was her business. I was her sister, not her mother."

"Was Timothy in love with her?"

"Were you?" A sneer crossed Jenny's lips.

Rowan ran his tongue over his cracked molar. "Who was the next member cast?"

"Edward. He was a natural and he obeyed without question. Every once in a while you find an actor like that. Everything that comes out of his mouth sounds authentic. I fell in love the moment I heard him read."

"And Maura?"

"You saw the first few scenes. I needed a brat."

Rowan nodded. "She had experience?"

"She said she did, but I doubted it."

"In Ohio?"

"I thought it was Iowa."

"Did you know a man named Clarence Williams?"

Jenny's spine straightened. The breath from her mouth became audible. "I...I believe I met him once or twice, yes."

"What was he like?"

"Why are you asking me this?"

"Because I believe your sister's murder was connected with the death of Clarence Williams twenty-three years ago."

Jenny's mouth remained a grim line above her chin. "How?"

"What was he like?"

She paced opposite him, their eyes only meeting when they crossed each other in the middle of the room. "Um...he was the kind of man my sister was attracted to, an uncomplicated man." Her eyes darted over the floor searching for something. "He worked at a steel mill, the one near McCormick."

Lost a bit of bumptiousness, have we? "After his body was found, the police drove Lisa up to Devil's Lake."

"Baraboo, if I remember correctly," Jenny said softly.

"Lisa was Clarence's girlfriend?"

"Clarence had a lot of girlfriends. My sister was just one of them."

"Did she know that?" asked Rowan. He was barely giving her time to finish the answers.

"If she wasn't lying to herself, she did."

"A witness said Lisa was not the woman driving north with Clarence when he was killed. In fact, the witness gave a description of the woman whom she saw."

"Really?"

"It was a rotund blonde. A smoker."

Jenny stopped to take a drag. "Fascinating."

"Was your sister nervous when she went to Baraboo?"

"Of course not."

Rowan moved directly in front of her. "Yes, of course not. She had not done anything, so why would she have cause to be nervous?"

"Is there something you wish to say to me, detective? Something that isn't subtextual?"

"Were you jealous of your sister?"

"I always was. Lisa was perfect."

"Were you jealous of Clarence Williams?"

"Yes. He wanted my sister to marry him."

"Did you ever sleep with him?"

Jenny paused. "He seduced me once, when I was in the mood to be seduced."

Rowan nodded. "And then he went back to Lisa and you were left alone, abandoned."

"It's plausible. But why would I wait twenty-three years and then kill my sister?"

"Have you already made an appointment to receive your sister's inheritance?"

"Friday the twelfth. It's not a crime to inherit money."

Rowan marched to the coffee table and drank the full cup of tea in one swig. "Which brand is this?"

Jenny stammered. "Millstone."

"Never heard of it. It is superb."

"It's the most common tea there is."

"Would you make me one more cup before I depart?" he asked with a smile.

"I think you've drunk enough tea, detective."

"Oh, but...perhaps you could give me a single bag for the road. I believe Williams would love this tea."

Jenny waddled toward the kitchen, a disgusted look on her face. When she disappeared around the corner, Rowan grabbed a souvenir and ran out the door.

Walter washed the dust out of two glasses. He poured three fingers of whisky in each one. Rowan spoke into the telephone with a dulcet tone. "I'm a friend of the family."

The nurse's voice came through the receiver in a distant, grating whine. "I fully understand everything you have said, Mr. Manory. Perhaps you could extend me the same courtesy. It is impossible for me to give patient information over the telephone. I certainly cannot dole it out willy-nilly to an unrelated *friend* such as yourself."

Rowan's hand scrunched the top page of the newspaper, but his voice retained the same measured calm. "Madam, her sister is recently deceased, and I need to contact Miss Pluviam to inform her of this dreadful news. As you should have surmised by now, it is quite urgent. All I need to know is if she was ever a patient at your hospital and—"

"This conversation is just about over."

"Fine, fine. May I speak with the head of orthopedic surgery then?"

"Not in today."

"Could you please give him my name and telephone number, and ask him to call me?" She wrote down the information and hung up. Rowan slammed the receiver. "Nitwit."

Walter said, "Come now, Manory. The poor woman's only doing her job."

"Lives are at stake, Williams."

"She doesn't know that. You have to convince her. You'll get more honey from a bee if you...no, that's not right. You'll get more honey from a bear—"

"You catch more flies with honey than with vinegar."

Walter snapped his fingers. "That's it. Take me, for example. How do you think I get my information?"

"Bribery. You pay them off," said Rowan.

"That is only part of it, my friend. Charm is the key. Secretaries are among the most underappreciated members of society."

Rowan laid out a cigarette paper on the desk. "She was a nurse."

"Regardless. She answers telephones. All day long, people call her, demanding information. She is taken for granted. The only thing she wants in this world is for someone to take the time to make her feel special. It's all anybody really wants. Tell her she has pretty legs."

"Over the phone?"

"Adapt. Tell her she has a beautiful voice."

"In this case, impossible. The woman would know I was lying."

Walter unwrapped his sardolive. "Why do you want to talk to the doctor anyway? Do you think she's lying about how she lost her hand?"

"She's lying about something. Every single one of them is lying about something." Rowan inhaled the acrid scent of the Dreighton and, with an unsteady grasp, poured it down his throat. "After my chat with Miss Pluviam, I went to the iron mill near McCormick where Clarence used to work."

Walter cleaned his ear with his pinkie. "That was a long time ago. Does anyone from back in the day still work there?"

Rowan nodded. "An elderly Polack named Andre. He and Clarence used to share drinks and occasionally other things."

"Did he give you any useful information?"

"Andre told me that he and Clarence used to spend time at a woman's house, 1235 Crenshaw."

"Crenshaw? That's in the black belt."

"That makes sense. The woman was a Negro."

"You think she's still alive?" asked Walter.

"Andre did not know. As he so colorfully told me, the rooster stopped crowing long ago. I also went to the hospital to inquire about our friend, Edward. Wouldn't you know it, he has been fired."

"Ooohh, the plot thickens." Walter bit into the sardolive.

"The nurse would not tell me the reason for his dismissal, so I may have to get Grady to call them on my behalf. Speaking of Grady." Rowan took out his souvenir from the desk.

"What have you got there?"

"Jenny and Lisa Pluviam's senior yearbook. If Grady comes

through with the address in Baraboo, I will have a photograph of Jenny to show the eyewitness."

"You had more fun than I did. I spent my day talking on the telephone and walking around apartment buildings." Walter wiped egg yolk off his face and referenced his notes. "Based solely on the interviews, we have one *proven* liar."

"Miss Lewis," Rowan said with confidence.

"There is a Trenton in Ohio, but none of the Lewis families in Trenton know anyone named Maura. The current address she gave the cops was bogus, too. There's no Stratton Street in Chicago."

"That is why she did not want to tell us her address. Maura had invented a street for the police and could no longer remember her fabrication when speaking with us. What about Edward?"

"Born to Agatha Filius. No father listed on the birth certificate. His aunt was declared the legal guardian when the mother was committed to Chester State Hospital. Don't be fooled by the name; it's a loony bin. She died there when he was three. Sepsis."

"Does his address check out?" asked Rowan.

Walter nodded. "Uh-huh. I walked through the alley. Dracula-looking old lady in the back window. Must have been his Aunt Christine."

"Timothy?"

"His father is a chemist. Dr. Edmond Brown. Mother's deceased. Has six sisters, all scientists of one kind or another."

"Timmy is the black sheep."

"I went over to his apartment, talked to his neighbor. He hasn't been home since Saturday. I'll keep trying to find another address."

"Perhaps Allison wised up and kicked him out."

"Allison checks out completely. She lived at the McGraw Orphanage until she was eighteen. The dean of the Goodman School gave her a scholarship. He chooses an orphan every year."

Rowan nodded slowly. "That leaves one." He tapped Grizz's photo on the front page of the Tribune. "Unfortunately, he has gone into hiding."

Walter grinned. "I have some good news on that front. Grizz has the apartment on Wilson, but that place is staked out. Good-looking, fit men in suits—definitely not cops. There's no chance for me to search the place. But, I got another address about an hour ago from Jimmy Dykes."

"Dykes, Dykes..." Rowan's eyebrows shot up. "The State Fair Flasher?"

Walter frowned. "Good God, a guy shows up to the state fair with nothing but a raincoat one time, and the poor fellow is forever known as *The* State Fair Flasher. Jimmy is Grizz's cousin. He gave me an address for a different place, said Grizz never stays there. I drove by and there were no agents outside, not yet anyway. I'll go tomorrow and see what's what."

"Take Young with you."

Walter's eyes narrowed. "What?"

"You heard me. He's still working the Polish neighborhood. Find him and say Grady ordered him to go with you."

"What if the kid gets in trouble?"

"Mr. Thompson is responsible for the deaths of eight people, possibly nine. It will be dangerous. If I were to lose you, there would be no one to make the coffee."

Walter swirled the ice in his glass. "I got a stupid question."

"Have at it."

"Where exactly are we going with the investigation?"

Rowan took a heavy breath. "I am currently juggling the focus. Jenny was my first instinct. One always must follow the money, and no one benefits more from Lisa's death. That business on the catwalk leads me to believe she was working with Grizz."

"And why would they write a death threat?"

"I have been thinking about that too. Do you recall the Lasciva case?"

Walter nodded. "I think about Lasciva every time it rains."

"That case had some startling similarities to our current one. A simple death threat was received. While we moronically pondered the motives of the killer, we failed to see the result of the threat."

"You mean..." Walter held up a finger before dropping it. "I was going to hazard a guess, but I'm afraid I have no idea what you mean, Manory."

"The result, my dear Williams, was that we were baited into going to Mississippi. Now," Rowan poured a second glass, "what was the result of the Pluviam death threat?"

"Same thing, I suppose. But, no one tried to kill us this time. Or did they? Have I missed something?"

"I have a funny feeling you and I were meant to be witnesses to Lisa's death."

"I have to disagree with you there, boss. The killer didn't need witnesses. There were plenty of them, two hundred paying ones, in fact."

"True, Williams, but none of the audience members knew the circumstances. You and I had intimate knowledge of the scenario, the cast, the theater. We knew what was coming, and we could not provide a solution to the murder nor prove that one even existed. It could have been an invaluable resource for the murderer, far better than a simple alibi. If we could not solve the murder, no one could."

"How would it work though? I can't even imagine…"

"It wouldn't. Unless…" A piece of the puzzle appeared in Rowan's mind, but he quickly stowed it away, fearful of its implications.

"Unless what?"

"Nothing. There are other possibilities of course. One on which I am quite keen involves Clarence Williams. All the actors are old enough to be his child. If his offspring were seeking revenge—"

"But Lisa didn't kill Clarence. They took her to Baraboo and the witness said she didn't do it. It wouldn't be revenge."

"The killer may not know that. Or perhaps the killer knows something we do not. If this theory is correct, then we have three suspects."

"You mean four."

"I mean what I said. Timothy Brown has a father. Naturally, he would be excluded."

"Now just a second, boss. What if Timothy was angry about Lisa breaking up with him? You saw how unhinged he was in Lisa's office. I thought he was going to strangle you."

"This would be the third theory and the one that satisfies me the least. Love is a strong motive for murder, but Timothy seemed the most troubled by her death. I don't believe Mr. Brown wanted Lisa Pluviam dead. But all this conjecture is neither here nor there. Things will become clearer once I get the address in Baraboo. Somehow, Clarence is the key. I'm sure of it." Rowan balled up the empty cigarette paper and threw it on the floor.

"What's wrong, Manory?"

"I fear that everything I need to solve this case has already been presented to me. The Rowan Manory of yesteryear would have cracked this nut by now. At the very least, he would have known exactly which of those three threads to follow."

"California, boss. The sunshine and the girls will fix your brain right up."

"I doubt it, Williams. The train has left the station." Rowan raised a wobbly glass. The ice jangled like tiny bells. "Here is to the man I once was."

Walter clinked his whiskey against Rowan's. "I never liked that guy anyway. Such a damn know-it-all."

While the detectives sat drinking in their office, a get-together was happening across town, one which would present to them a most irregular piece of the puzzle.

8

DAVID BROUTHERS'S SHINDIG

10:37 p.m. Tuesday, April 9th

Fractured structural cracks zigzagged across the steps and walls, rising up to the fifth floor along the wide, alabaster stairway. Evidence of past gatherings lay strewn about in the form of confetti, paper hats, and an unmistakable whiff of dried urine. The doors of the lower apartments hung open, some of them torn from the hinges and leaning against the walls. A cacophony of giggles, moans, and orgiastic screams came from within the rooms, suggesting some of the partygoers preferred solitude for their activities.

Edward stopped at the base of the fourth floor and pulled

Maura toward him, lifting her bottom so they could kiss. A couple passed them down the steps, stopping to give a playful *tsk tsk*.

Maura settled her buck teeth on her lower lip and straightened Edward's tie. "This is going to be fun. You've never seen anything like a David Brouthers shindig."

"Yeah, you keep telling me. I think you may have oversold this thing."

"I collect stories from these parties."

"Are they going in the act too?"

Maura widened her eyes and nodded. "I like to think of myself an art journalist when I come here, taking notes on the sordid underbelly of the artistic community. That's what David calls it anywho. I'm not sure why it's an underbelly."

Edward wrinkled his nose. "What's that smell?"

"Reefer. They'll offer it to you. Don't smoke it."

"No worries. I won't go near it."

A woman in an undraped kimono answered the door. She was naked underneath, and the sides of her garment hung loosely on her arms. "Maura, darling." She leaned forward and kissed the air around Maura's cheeks. "Who's the fly in the fucksuit?"

Edward said, "Pardon?"

Maura slapped his shoulder. "This is Eddie. He was in the play with me."

The woman gasped. "The one where the actress bought the farm? That must have been wild. Did you see her die?"

Edward stared at her breasts. "No, I...My name's Edward."

"I heard." She extended her hand. "I'm Juliette. I was named after the de Sade heroine."

Edward finally looked at her face, hypnotized by the single false eyelash constantly fluttering above her right eye. "Who's de Sade?"

"The Marquis."

"Never met him."

"Very progressive man, very Parisian. I was born in Paris."

Juliette opened the door wide and beckoned them to enter the crowded kitchen. Five or six groups stood together drinking, wildly yelling over the din from the living room. Maura nodded to a man wearing a sailor suit with a beer under his tattooed arm. A Filipino woman moved from group to group asking where Billy was. Three identical women in black flapper dresses took turns kissing each other. Their skin was white as porcelain.

Maura pulled Edward against the counter by his tie. "Put your tongue back in your mouth."

"What's wrong with these people?" asked Edward.

"They're actors, Ed. It's a big show."

"Why is Juliette naked?"

"Her name is Ethel. She lives in the suburbs and her dad's a bank clerk. She's just high." The entryway to the living room was clogged with strangers trying to push in both directions. The sound of feet pounding out the jitterbug rag vibrated through the walls. Maura leaned in close to his ear. "Get us a couple drinks and meet me in the living room. I have to go talk to David."

Edward yanked her forward. "Alone?"

"Oh, God." Maura ran her hands up and down his chest. "You're so ginchy when you're jealous."

"I am?"

"I'll be a good girl, don't you worry." Their lips touched with a sticky, languid kiss, and she bounced off him, bending her way through the packed crowd into the living room.

Edward stood unnaturally still in the corner of the kitchen. No one had ever called him ginchy. An older Italian woman with green eyes and the hint of a mustache asked him if he was a business man. He proudly replied that he was an actor, and he was here with his girlfriend.

In the living room, the music from the record player drowned out attempts at conversation. Smoke wafted in billows under the lampshades. Maura pushed her way through, peeling her shoes off the sticky wooden floor with every step. She screamed at a few people, asking where David was. A real, honest-to-God descendent of the Meskwaki Tribe pointed a spear at the glass door to the balcony.

David Brouthers was outside, leaning over the rail so far that his feet were off the ground. Maura closed the door behind her and yelled out, "Don't jump!"

"Shut up." Brouthers pointed downward over the rail. "Look." A homeless man was lying prone, half of his body on the sidewalk and the other half in the street. He stared intently at the figure. "He hasn't moved. I think he's dead"

Maura squinted at the street. "He's probably sleeping."

"Nah. He's dead." Brouthers lifted a whiskey glass high in the air and let it drop. The glass missed its target by a few feet, but the shatter woke the man up with a start. Brouthers's mouth gaped. "Go figure. I guess you were right. He's not dead after all."

Maura's fists hit her thighs. "David, you could have killed him!"

Brouthers turned, recognizing her freckled face. "Maura. Thank God you're here." He lifted her with a bear hug and spun her. "Did you bring the morphine?"

"No."

"Oh, baby. I could have used it tonight. I'm almost out." Brouthers pouted. "What happened?"

"Jeez Louise." Maura pushed her way out of the hug. "My line quit his job. I couldn't get any more."

"Delivery boy quit? He's gotta get his job back. Or maybe he knows somebody that still works there. I got plenty of duff, but it's not like what you brought. That was the real thing—hospital grade."

"I'll ask him."

"If he quit, then he probably needs money. Everyone needs money." Brouthers looked down at the screaming bum. "You need money, right? Can you get me some proper morphine, sir?"

Maura took Brouthers by the jaw, turning his head toward her. "My friend doesn't need money. And if you talk to him, don't say anything about it."

"Why the hell not?"

"He doesn't know I took it."

"You little minx." He gave her backside a sharp pinch. "Oh, another one of your friends is here."

"Allie came?"

"No, Tim. That guy is a madman." Brouthers laughed. "First he drank a bottle of champagne and then he inhaled more Benzedrine than any human being I've ever seen." He stopped talking, unnerved by an unfamiliar look of dread staring back at him. "What?"

"Where is Tim?"

"I don't know." Brouthers looked back at the bum. "Maybe that's him. Hey! Is your name Tim?"

Back in the kitchen, Edward found two glasses and played eeny, meeny, miney, mo with the liquor, ending up on a bottle of Calvert. A knock came at the front door. No one seemed to be in a rush to answer it, so he pulled on the handle. Allison stood in the hall, appearing so weary and anemic it pained Edward to even look at her. "Allie."

Her words came out hoarsely with put upon joy. "Hiya, Eddie. It's good to see you." Allison's embrace was awkward, her hands galumphing against his body for support.

Edward felt her cheek, cold and blubbery against his skin. "I'm glad you came. We missed you."

Allison's pupils dilated a bit when she looked round the kitchen, her head bopping to the music. "How's the party?"

"Yeah, it's…it's hopping. Let's see." Edward pointed to the corner. "That guy in the vest, he's Sam. He's a phantom engineer. He'll look into your soul and fix your karmatic something or other. And there was a psychic here before, but he passed out, and his friends dragged him down the stairs. Didn't see it coming, I guess."

Allison grabbed a random glass off the counter and downed it.

Edward snatched the empty glass from her hand. "Whoa! You don't want to do that. Maura said the drinks are probably spiked."

She put her mouth against Edward's ear. "Good." She grabbed another drink and repeated it. Warmth seeped through her body and a bit of rose color appeared on her face. When Maura forced her way into the kitchen, Allison raised her arms in celebration. "The gang's all here."

Maura grabbed hold of Allie's hands. She spoke breathlessly. "Allie, we have to go."

Edward said, "Why?"

Allison wrinkled her brow. "Go? Ridiculous. We're not going anywhere. Are we, Eddie?"

Maura pleaded with her. "It was a mistake to come. I didn't realize how crazy it would be. You can't even talk to anyone. And it's boring, anywho. We could go to a bar."

Allison huffed. "We'll go somewhere and pay for drinks that we can get for free? Relax, dollface." She grabbed Edward's drink and hustled into the crowd.

Edward pulled Maura aside. "Why do we have to leave?"

Maura said, "Tim's here, and he's buttered to the gills."

"*Oh, drat.*" His face blanched. "That's bad."

"I'll get Allie, pull her onto the balcony before she sees him. You find Tim and take him home. Not home home, just wherever he came from."

"But—"

A scream erupted from the living room. With a crash of the record player, the music stopped. Allison had Juliette by the hair, the locks twisted tightly in her fists. Timothy slumbered against the wall with his pants around his ankles, barely cognizant of the fight in front of him. Juliette broke free and ran out the front door with her hands covering the scratches on her face. Allison dug bloody, chewed nails into her palms. Her flame-lit eyes regarded Timothy with a tipsy cunning.

He slobbered as he spoke. "Babe, I didn't see you come in. You here to finish the job?"

"So smart. So goddamn smart." The words ground through her clenched teeth. "We'll see who's smart after I go to the police."

Timothy reached out to grab her arm, but she easily avoided his grasp. "Get a grip of yourself. You're causing a scene."

"I know how you did it. I know how you killed Lisa."

He snickered. "You're crazy. Always been crazy. And I done had to put up with it."

Mumbled voices from the room came out like a backing chorus in a play.

"Allison's talking about that actress."

"Timothy killed her?"

"I thought she fell."

Allison cried drearily, her tough exterior cracking. "I thought you did it for me. That's why I didn't tell anyone. That's why I hid the evidence. But not anymore, Timmy. I've got it hidden away where you can't find it. You're going to sit on the hotsquat, and I'm going to watch you fry from a front-row seat."

Timothy leaned his head back against the wall. "Fine," he drawled. "You do that. Tell the police everything you know. Just lemme walk you home. You're not well. It ain't safe out there."

"I was going to get rid of it, but I kept it. Just in case. I'll take it to that detective in the morning. He'll believe me." Allison flounced off, sobbing through the kitchen with Maura running after her.

Edward approached Timothy cautiously. The crowd milled about in the background, unsure of what to do next. The chatter died down, and a jarring silence took over the room. "Go easy, Tim. It's me. I'm your friend, remember."

"I'm in trouble, Eddie."

"What did you do?" Edward stared at Timothy's hands, leery of a sudden attack.

"Done did something that can't be undone. Why am I so stupid?" Timothy slapped his own face three times in a row, leaving bright red welts across his cheek.

"Don't do that. Let me take you home. You want to go to sleep, don't you?"

151

"Lisa used me." His mouth twisted, rage appearing in his voice. "I loved her, Ed. Jesus, I sound like a goddamn swish. I'm not supposed to be this way, am I? I'm supposed to be a man." Timothy punched against the wall and then whimpered, "I might as well kill Allie too. What's one more body?"

Edward held his hands out, patting the air between them. "It's okay, Tim. A good night's sleep is all you need. You're just confused. In the morning, everything will make sense."

A shotgun blast exploded from behind. The projectiles hit the ceiling, raining plaster over the living room. Ducking and screaming, the remaining party members squeezed into the kitchen and then scrambled down the stairs.

Brouthers pointed the shotgun at Edward. "Are you the pill who broke my record player?"

Edward stood shaking, his hands raised in surrender. "No. I'm Maura's friend."

Brouthers grinned at him and lowered the shotgun. "Well, well, well. If it isn't mister morphine."

Edward looked back to the wall. Timothy wasn't there. Allison and Maura had left. The guests were gone. Edward was all alone with David Brouthers.

The hot breeze began as gentle susurrations, but as midnight passed and Allison crossed a lonely intersection, it became a fierce, rustling rush of heat. The spindly trees along the sidewalk bent, their leaves flickering back and forth against the bark like ticker tape.

The air lashed against Allison's face. Beads of sweat dribbled on her chest before falling chilly onto her sternum and finally seeping into the cotton fabric of her dress. The sounds of footsteps on the pavement could be heard between the whirring whistle of the air. Or was it an auditory illusion? Every time she looked back, there was no one following her.

"Hello?" she yelled.

A traffic cone sputtered from around the corner and was swept along the street, flipping over several times before wedging itself into a storm drain. She kicked off her heels, slowly bending down to pick them up. "Go to hell, Tim!" After a few stumbling, backward steps, she decided to run. Her thighs grew tired and sore after a single block, turning the last stretch into a staggering, gasp-filled trot. *Jesus, help me.*

She turned one more corner and slammed into the glass door of The Red Rising Theater. The keys fumbled from her handbag, slippery and clanging against one another. They fell from her grasp. *No. No.* The sound of her pulse throbbed in her ears as every movement slowed down. The key butted against the lock, refusing to go in. *Fiddlesticks.*

The sweet release of the door's tension reverberated through her hand. She slammed the door shut and pressed her quivering face against the glass, her see-saw breath creating a mild fog. All she could see was the empty Chicago street. No one was out there. Her muscles slowly expanded. A scared little laugh came from her belly. *Foolish 'til the end.*

The power in the Red Rising Theater had been shut off since Sunday. It was usually such a bustling space, actors going back and forth in various stages of dress, grips measuring and hammering, and the husky shouts of Jenny echoing about. Now abandoned and quiet, the building struck Allison as eerie and forlorn, wholly unnatural.

She stumbled to the ticket booth, her hands waving blindly above the bottom shelf. *Horus smoked. He's got to have a few lighters stashed down here.* She found a Colibri that still worked. The light vibrated along the narrow hallway, a flickering red above a solid blue flame. The guts of the building groaned in the background. It was one of those noises that empty buildings made from pockets of air or the contraction of wood or some other such scientific explanation.

A dry, faded bloodstain covered the floor underneath the still-erect balcony. The curtain was fully drawn, exposing the crossover along with the entrance to the wing.

While she walked to the dressing room, Allison had the vague notion she was dreaming. She pinched her leg. *Why would that work? Why would a pinch wake me up? It's a dream pinch. It isn't real.*

She flipped the lighter shut, setting it on the chest of drawers and then fumbled around in the dark in search of the bottom drawer's knobs. She pulled it off its hinges with a short little pop, exposing the floor underneath. Her hand stretched into the corner as far as it could without quite reaching what she was looking for. Allison lay flat, wiggling her fingers along the ground. The lighter fell off the top of the dresser, scattering across the room and smacking into something. *Shoot.* The tip of her nail brushed against some tissue paper. *That's it.* She secured the edge of the tissue between two fingers. Her hand pulled out in a fist. In her grasp was proof of murder.

After a long, frustrating search, Allison found the lighter. A few clicks of the button and the flame caught, its wavering reflection glowing in her wet eyes. *What if Tim is waiting at the apartment? I'll go to Eddie. He'll help me. His address must be in Jenny's office.*

About half way down the wing, Allison noticed a light dancing in odd, widening arcs. As she got closer, one hand gliding along the wall, the light grew bigger and began to shimmer with more movement. At about five feet, she could see the face above the light. It had a grin so wide both rows of teeth showed. Allison looked into eyes she had seen many times before. They morphed into the eyes of a stranger. With dawning fright, she looked back down at the light and saw it was not a light, but rather a reflection of the Colibri's flame—an evil, sinister reflection in the blade of a razor.

9

WHAT YOU DON'T KNOW GETS YOU KILLED

Murder is a curious affair. To look at someone and say 'you shall breathe nevermore' requires a level of passion I would not think the human mind capable. Reality provides ample evidence to the contrary. Not only are people capable, but given the opportunity, they are inclined. Passion was at the heart of Lisa's murder. I cannot solve how it was committed...not yet anyway. Perhaps I can discover from which heart this passion lies buried.

Rowan sucked in his gut, barely buttoning his trousers before letting the paunch expand over the waistline. His pallid, craggy hands slung a tie around his upturned collar.

Jenny was so distraught when it happened. Days later, she reverted to viciousness. It is self-defense. A woman like that, a damaged, bitter shell, must protect herself. It seems Grizz is capable of murder, but this one? It does not feel right. Mr. Thompson is a foot soldier. Why would a delivery driver be fired? Edward was either late or stealing his shipment. Why is Maura afraid of the police? Is her fear convergent or parallel to Lisa's murder? Timothy's passion lies on the surface. It is not in a murderer's best interest to play his hand like that...unless he is doubly cunning. Allison knows something. She must. Why else would she—

The telephone rang from Williams's desk. Rowan's hands held tightly onto the ends of the tie. "How...How to tie a Windsor?" *I have performed this simple action countless times.* His hands twisted the tail and the blade in every possible direction and combination. Nothing was recognizable to him. "Oh, God. I am losing my mind." Rowan dropped the tie to his feet and stumbled out to the phone.

Grady's voice rasped with shell-shocked solemnity. "You'd better get down to The Red Rising Theater, Manory."

"There has been another murder."

"Just get down here."

The signs of the city's despair moved left to right through the cab's window. *Free coffee for the unemployed. No Micks, No Wops, No Armenians. Death to the Bourgeoisie. Four children for sale–Inquire within. Closed.* Most of the buildings were closed. People stood beside empty storefronts, broken glass lying about the sidewalk under their feet. A burning stench drifted through the air without an identifiable source.

Entertainment and death are the only remaining enterprises, and business is booming. I did not expect another murder. Not so soon. The second murder is always different from the first. It is one of those lessons you learn and then quickly forget.

Rowan pulled the tie from his pocket. He closed his eyes. *Over, under, up, and through. Success.* His head fell back onto the seat. *Today I forget a knot. Tomorrow, my name. And there will come a day, sooner than I realize, when a stranger will be staring back in the mirror. Everything I have spent my life building will vanish. The only thing remaining will be the cold, looming specter of death.*

"Twenty."

Rowan snapped back to consciousness. "Pardon?"

The hack looked at him through the rearview mirror. "We're at the theater, pops. Twenty cents."

The cop stationed at the theater door extended a bully club toward Rowan's chest. "Move along, Frankenstein. Ain't nothing to see here."

"I am Rowan Manory. Sergeant Grady is expecting me."

"Oh. Sorry. I gotta be careful. We've had photographers trying to get in here. They can smell a good story."

"It comes with the job I suppose."

"No, I mean literally. If you stand outside the fire escape, you can smell it. I had to give a couple of the rats a shiner."

"Have you seen the body?"

"Uh-uh." The cop leaned in close and whispered. "But it smells like shit mixed with meat back there. Whatever happened, it ain't good, and we're to keep it under wraps."

Grady was sitting in the front row with a hat flopped over his knee. Rowan had never seen him look so contemptuous, so utterly defeated. "Come on, she's in the dressing room. Brace yourself."

"I have seen it before," said Rowan.

The sergeant shook his head. "Not this you ain't. Even I ain't seen this before. We got a nutter on our hands, the kind that gets studied by eggheads in white rooms."

The flashing of camera bulbs and the cracking of glass came from the doorway. The cold, heavy smell of rot overtook the air in the wing. It swept to the back of Rowan's throat. He raised his velum. Grady stopped to cross himself before entering.

Allison's body lay sprawled against the chest of drawers, both palms turned toward the ceiling. The final moment of horror was etched on her face.

Rowan knelt in front of the corpse. "Do you believe me now, Grady?"

The sergeant pursed his lips. "We don't know for sure if this is connected to Pluviam. It's still speculation. I sent men to find the cast and question them as to their whereabouts on Tuesday night."

"To my eyes, it appears that two separate weapons were used, yes?"

Grady nodded. "As far as we can tell, a straight razor was used on the throat and then a kitchen knife…Is that right, Davis, a kitchen knife?"

Davis, a short, ghoulish man with fat cheeks and bloody, pale-green rubber gloves, stood motionless in the corner. "I said it looks that way. Don't quote me 'til we get her to McKinley in post."

"In all probability, a kitchen knife was used to do…" Grady pointed at the body. "…that."

Rowan tilted his head at the blank space where the drawer had been pulled out. "What did the cast have to say?"

"We haven't been able to locate Maura Lewis or Timothy Brown yet. Jenny Pluviam and Edward Filius were cooperative, but neither has an alibi. There are no prints and we don't have either weapon although we do have a good idea where the razor came from."

"Do you have a working motive?"

"Yeah, a pretty damn good one if you ask me. Timothy Brown and the victim were at a party last night. Scummy little bug named Brouthers threw it. Witnesses saw them fighting. Allison seemed to implicate him in Lisa Pluviam's death. Maura Lewis and Edward Filius were there as well. We're treating this as a crime of passion."

And yet, it is clearly the opposite. Rowan stood. "What's this about the murder weapon?"

Grady sucked his teeth at the only good piece of news. "It's likely from the bathroom of the victim's apartment. We found Timothy Brown's shaving case minus the razor."

"How convenient."

"What do you mean, *how convenient*?"

Rowan patted his forehead with a handkerchief. "The faster you get me the address I asked for, the faster I will know what's happening."

"But Brown's the man, yeah? Somebody strong had to do this, right Davis?"

"Ask McKinley."

Rowan lit a sloppily rolled cigarette. The loose paper erupted into a large flame. He stamped it out under his shoe. "Who found the body?"

"Jenny Pluviam."

"May I speak with her?"

Grady shook his head. "We took her back home. Imagine walking in on this without warning. She's in shock." He looked back at the wing. "Where's your buddy?"

Walter whistled as he skipped up the stairs, the melodic sweetness of Gene Austin's vocal playing in his head. *There she is. There she is. That's what keeps me up at night. Oh Gee whiz, Oh Gee whiz. That's why I can't eat a bite. Now ain't she sweet? See her coming down the street. I ask you confidentially, ain't she sweet?*

The blades of the hall's window fan whooshed like a windmill struggling to keep pace with a tempest. Crimson walls surrounded a crimson carpet with only the tarnished brass of the door numbers ruining the monochromous red. The fan's deformed shadow stretched the length of the hallway.

Apartment 304. A small tap of his knuckle went unanswered. When a more strident knock yielded the same result, Walter rapped at the door with full force.

The door cracked open and a woman stuck out her nose. Her speech was marred by a stiff bottom lip, perhaps the result of a stroke or two. "Can I help you, sir?" She opened the door a bit wider. Although the bones of her face had retained their firm youthful shape, her skin had sagged around that still imposing structure, giving her a constant disapproving look.

Now, that is a biddy—a woman dying to be played with. A gigantic Maine Coon emerged, rubbing its face against the woman's calves. Walter knelt onto the dirty floor like a child playing on a rug. "What an adorable kitty. Is it a he or a she?"

"It's a he. That's Mr. Jinx. He's the resident troublemaker." She reached down and scratched the cat's chin. It responded with a soulful, high-pitched mew.

" Aww, Mr. Jinx looks like a tiger, but he sounds like a little girl. What's the breed?"

"Pure Coon. He's terribly friendly."

"May I pet him?"

She gave the goofiest of misshapen grins.

Walter held out his hand, snapping his fingers. "Puss, puss. Puss, puss."

Mr. Jinx rolled into the hallway, its paws pointed straight up, exposing a furry belly. The woman clasped her hands together under her chin. "That's his invitation to play. Jinxy doesn't do that for everyone. He must like you. It's a gift to be liked by a cat; they're very particular creatures."

As Walter rubbed Jinx's belly, its eyes dilated and its limbs closed on his arm like a trap. The front claws dug into his wrist while the back ones ripped into the sleeve with a series of rabbit kicks. Walter tried to yank his arm away, but the cat's grip kept him in place. "Takes it rather seriously, doesn't he?"

"When my husband ain't home, the fuzzy monster hasn't got anyone to play with. Got a lot of aggression, he does. Refuses to take it out on me, bless his little heart."

Distracting the cat with his left hand, Walter managed to free himself from its clutches. "Madam—"

She corrected him. "Shirley Bridge."

Dots of blood swelled over the scratches on his wrist. "Shirley, my name is Walter Williams. I am looking for the landlord of the premises."

Shirley stood a bit straighter. "Well, like I implied earlier, my husband ain't home. But I'm the landlady."

"Thank goodness. I much prefer landladies to landlords. They're so much more pleasant to look at."

She cocked her head, birdlike. "What can I do for you, Walter?"

"I was trying to get in touch with an old friend, a Mr.

Thompson."

Shirley put her nose in the air. "Ain't no Mr. Thompson who lives here."

"Perhaps you know him as *Grizz*?"

She frowned. "Oh, Grizzy. What you want with him?"

"I haven't seen Grizzy for ages. I don't even know what he's doing with himself these days, but I found out his address and came to say hello. I knocked on his door downstairs, but he doesn't seem to be home."

"Grizzy is a very busy man. Comes in and out a lot, but he keeps to himself, so I can't say what he does."

"Anything you could tell me about my friend would be most helpful."

She clucked her tongue. "He's not your friend, is he?"

Walter's face dropped from character. "How did you get to be so clever?"

"You should work for Cargill, Walter. I'm sure they have plenty of turkeys for you to butter up. But I ain't no turkey."

"No, you are not. I'm a private investigator." Walter gave her his card.

Shirley's hand trembled with excitement as she held it. "You investigating him then?"

"I suppose I am."

"Is Grizzy dangerous?"

"I don't know yet. That's why I'm here to ask him some questions. Perhaps I can ask you. Does Grizz stay here often?"

"No, he must sleep somewhere else." Shirley pushed her tongue against her cheek. "He does have meetings in that apartment though. European meetings."

"I don't understand. What do you mean by *European meetings?*"

"Strange-looking gentlemen, probably Jews. They call each other comrade."

Mr. Jinx took hold of Walter's ankle and bit through his sock. *Fucker.* "What do these Jews talk about?"

"I tried to listen, but they play the radio real loudlike and I can't make out their words. Political discussions from what I can muster. Yesterday, he left here with three men. I heard a bit of their conversation."

Walter leaned in close to the ever-widening crack in the door. "As I said, anything would be helpful."

"Grizzy said he could always go Southwest and get some more."

"Some more what?"

"Just some more."

"Hmmm. Southwest. That's rather cryptic."

"I thought so, too." Shirley folded her arms. "Why would he give a direction instead of naming a place like a normal person? I have a theory about where he was headed."

"Yes?"

"He calls it Southwest because he can't remember the name. It must be some little town no one's ever heard of."

"That's a fine deduction. Have you ever thought about becoming a detective, Shirley?"

"All the time. There's a lot of mystery in this here complex, and I'm privy to most of it. The scary part is what I don't know. Can't even tell how bad that is. What you don't know gets you killed."

"Quite right, quite right. Listen, I have to get going. If you see anything suspicious, give me a call." Walter extended a five dollar bill into Shirley's hand. "Remember, I was never here."

"Oh, I can't take that. It's too much."

Walter waggled his brows. "I want you to take this money and buy yourself something nice and what's more, I want you not to tell your husband. I want it to be a secret just between us."

Shirley tittered, lumbering backwards into her apartment with Mr. Jinx at her heels.

Walter hopped down to the second floor. A brilliant ray of light rested on the frame of door 209. *Probably a bad idea.* He inched along the hallway, the gyrations of the fan whipping louder with each step. *Definitely a bad idea.*

The ball pick slid easily into the lock with a click. Walter jimmied at the shear lines with a snake rake, finding them with ease. When the knob turned, he tapped the door open with a fingertip.

A single burnt-out bulb presided over the airless space under the low, cracked ceiling. The mattress, curled into the corner, didn't look like it was meant to be slept on. Walter's shoes stepped over uneven piles of papers and posters. He ripped a blanket from the window, letting in a bit of gray light from the back alley.

Two wooden folding doors signaled a closet on the right wall, and a door-less frame led to a rusty commode and an uninviting bathtub. There were no mirrors or toiletries.

Walter took off his suit coat and rolled up the sleeves of his shirt to sift through the mess. The posters were typical propaganda pieces, most of them featuring a demonic Uncle Sam in the process of raping a woman or wielding a whip over some terrified slaves in a cotton field. He looked them over casually, making a note of the address stamped on the backs. Among the empty cigarette packs and wads of tissue, he found a map of Illinois with various cities circled in red. Finally, Walter found exactly what he was looking for. *Oh, Grizz.* One of the newspapers was missing some of its letters. With a quick glance over the first few pages, he could nearly spell out *Lisa Pluviam on opening night you will die.* His pulse raced.

He searched for a hidden phone among the garbage. Walter had to tell Manory as soon as he could. He swept his hand blindly across the floor, revealing a pile of rat droppings. *Disgusting. How do you hold a meeting in a place like this? Can't even...The wire!*

He followed the wire from the wall as it vanished under some flannel shirts before appearing again and leading into the closet. Walter scurried to the closet doors and, right before pulling them open, had a notion he should have checked there first. *One should always secure a hostile location.* The idea had barely entered his head when the razor came slashing toward him.

The blade ripped across his outstretched hand just below the knuckles, flapping the flesh open. Blood spurted over his bowtie. He grabbed Grizz's arm and pulled him forward. The two men fell to the floor with Walter ending up on the bottom. Grizz was much stronger than he appeared. It wasn't muscle, but rather heavy bone that seemed to drive the razor toward Walter's right eye. He struggled in vain against Grizz's wrist, his wounded fingers burning with pain. Grizz gave a ferocious grunt along with invectives about Walter's mother as he pushed the red, rusty steel with both hands.

When the razor's edge covered his right eye's field of vision, Walter gambled. His head twisted to the left side as far as it could, and he pulled Grizz's hand down to the floor, driving the blade onto the wood. He pulled his legs forward and kicked the old man's ribs, sending him tumbling into the hall.

Walter slid back to the mattress, quickly wrapping a handkerchief around his mangled fingers. "Gaahh."

The furious pounding of Grizz's footsteps through the building was followed by the heavy thud of the front door. Then came the gunshot.

Young! Walter hustled down the stairs.

Outside, Officer Young stood trembling, the gun still pointed at Grizz's prone body on the ground.

Walter yelled, "Call an ambulance!"

Young remained still.

"Move it, kid!"

Young finally came back to his senses, holstering the gun and running to the café across the street.

Grizz leaned his head forward. The gaping wound in his chest let out a low pressurized hiss. "Oh, hell! Awww, come on!" He closed his mouth. When he opened it again, his teeth were red.

Walter kicked the razor across the lawn. He took hold of Grizz's hand. "Grizz, listen to me, there's an ambulance on the way. You're going to pull through. But, in case these are your last moments, I'll pray with you if you want. Would you like that, Grizz?"

"Go fuck..." He coughed. "...your dead mother...in hell."

"I'll take that as a *no*."

Grizz spat blood into his face. "This is how I go out?" A guttural wheeze came out from somewhere deep inside his body. Every word became strained. He squeezed Walter's good hand. "Looking at your ugly face?"

A crowd of tenants had gathered at the front door. Shirley Bridge yanked her window open and screamed for someone to call the police.

Walter wiped Grizz's blood from his eyes. "How did you kill her, Grizz? You don't want to take this to the grave. How did you kill Lisa Pluviam?"

Grizz sputtered a few more stertorous breaths before a trance-like serenity came over him. Walter kept asking the question as Grizz's gaze drifted upward, lost forever in the cloudless blue.

10

IT'S BLUNT, NOT OBVIOUS

12:03 p.m. Thursday, April 11th

"Where's Dave?"

The acne-ridden young man behind the bar cleared his throat. "My uncle asked me to open today, said he'd be here whenever he could get out of bed."

Rowan narrowed his eyes. "Is this legal—you working here at your age?"

"That depends. Are you a cop?"

"Excellent point. I'll have a brandy and," he sighed, "...a pack of Camels." Rowan watched the teenager stumble around the bar trying to find the combination of glass, liquor, and cigarettes.

Dave's nephew finally produced the goods. "Um...I'm not sure how much it is? Maybe twenty-five cents?"

"Sounds right. Just some friendly advice, don't pour the brandy to the rim of the glass...you want to..." Rowan pointed at the boy. "You are Dave's nephew."

"That's what I said."

"The one who hauls ashes."

"I...I..."

"Where did you hear the phrase?"

"Mister, I don't know what you're talking about."

"Was it from a film? Perhaps one of your friends?"

The nephew's voice cracked. "I think you should talk to my uncle. Whatever problem you got, I can't help you."

Rowan took a sip. "This tastes like vinegar."

"That's the only brandy on the shelf. Like I said, talk to Dave."

Walter strode into the Brown Bear, holding up his bandaged right hand. "You should see the other guy."

"Williams!" Rowan leapt from the chair to embrace his friend. "Oh, you stupid, sorry son of a bitch." He took hold of Walter's head with both hands. "Do not ever do that to me again."

"I can handle myself boss. I'm not a dame in front of a door. What are we drinking?" Walter took a sip from the glass. His lips jutted forward. "Tastes like piss. Hey kid, two Schlitze's. I'm buying one of them."

Rowan lit a Camel. "I tried to visit you in the hospital, but the

FBI would not allow it."

"Yeah, yeah, they gave me the third degree. I think they were just in a huff 'cause I found Grizz before they did. Where's Dave?"

"Never mind that. Tell me everything."

Walter relayed the meeting with Shirley Bridge and her crazy cat, the evidence in Grizz's apartment, and the shooting. "That settles it, Grizz killed her."

"You are sure about the letters."

"Pretty much letter for letter, boss. Grizz is the author."

Rowan squeezed the filter between his fingers. "And it was a razor he attacked you with?"

"Oh yeah. The bathroom had no lather or strop. It was definitely a weapon he carried with him."

"Yesterday was not good."

Walter licked the foam from his lips. "Did you have a tough time of it too?"

"Allison Miller has been murdered."

The smile left Walter's face. *"Oh, no."*

Rowan described the party and Allison's presumed journey to the dressing room. "Her throat was slit with a straight razor."

"So, let me get it straight. Grizz kills Lisa under Jenny's orders so she can get the inheritance. Grizz'll get a taste of it. Mind you, he's got this operation going while he's planning to bomb the Federal Building. Then he searches for some kind of evidence for this impossible murder that we can't figure out. Allison comes to get it, so he kills her. Then he calls Jenny and she comes in the next morning to report the body. That's the dumbass place our investigation has come to?"

"It gets worse." Rowan caught a look at himself in the mirror.

"Of course it does. Lay it on me."

"After Allison was murdered, her body was...defiled."

Walter paused. "I don't know what that means in this context."

"What I mean to say is the killer took the time to disembowel the corpse."

All the muscles in Walter's face went limp. "Why?"

Rowan leaned back in his chair, his head bobbing maniacally. "Exactly! Why would he do something like that? What purpose would it serve? I thought of little else last night while I lay in bed. Grady favors the psychological line of thought. But insanity is a lazy man's excuse."

"What exactly are we dealing with, Manory?"

"It is obvious."

"It's blunt, not obvious." Walter shook his head. "Allison had no family."

"Her death would eliminate any connection to Clarence Williams. Maura and Edward would become the prime suspects if the familial theory is correct."

Walter gave a helpless look to Rowan. "I just meant she has nobody to mourn for her. I'm sorry, I'll try to detach myself."

A rueful little shiver passed through Rowan. He quickly stowed it away. "Now is not the time to let emotions dominate our reasoning. The second murder is always done for a different reason than the first. This rule of thumb could not be more apparent than in this case. The murder of Lisa Pluviam was a perfect work of art. It was sophisticated and well-planned. We do not know how or why. Evidently, Allison Miller did. Somehow, the poor girl discovered something the killer knew would implicate him. Her murder was not planned. Despite its brutality, this act was far more impersonal than the opening night murder. It was not a crime of passion but rather, one of circumstance. I am not buying into Grizz as the killer just yet. It may simply seem that way."

"We're going in circles."

"Yes, but we are drifting inward. The right clue has yet to present itself."

"Do you think the killer might have wanted to make it seem like a different man killed Allison? A different style of murder might force us to take up new leads."

"That would be a far more likely explanation. The defilement of the corpse was almost certainly utilitarian in nature. It served some purpose."

"What's the next move?"

"Tomorrow, we will get the post mortem report from McKinley. *Your* next move is to go home. Take the rest of the day off."

"No chance, boss. This case is getting far too bloody. Wherever you go, I go."

"Do not worry, Williams. I will not be involved in anything dangerous. I am simply going to pay Althea Johnson a visit in the black belt."

"You aren't doing anything dangerous, but you're going into the black belt." He raised his glass. "Here's to paradoxes. Hey kid, get me another."

The nephew's mouth was agape. "Who the hell are you people?"

When the cab stopped at the corner of Crenshaw and Wilson, the hack warned Rowan about staying in the neighborhood too long after dark. "Whites who walk into the black belt don't always walk out if you know what I mean."

None of the blocks had a sidewalk and the apartment buildings were all pushed back at least thirty feet from the curb, the space in between consisting of dirt and garbage. Rats scurried over splintered wooden planks in search of food. There were no shops or restaurants in sight, only the distant downtown buildings, covered in haze like some dream of civilization.

Nearly sixty doors covered the side of the apartment building, packed in tightly across four flights. Wooden stairways ran along jagged, uneven angles. Collapse of the whole structure seemed imminent.

A little girl with a charcoal-painted doll opened her door. She leaned over a second-level stairway.

Rowan bowed. "Good evening."

She didn't smile. "Hello."

"Perhaps you could help me."

"There ain't nobody home."

He scanned all the doors. "No one here but you?"

"They at the Sunset. Only children and old folks here."

"Excellent. I'm looking for the latter."

"We have stairs. No ladders."

"I am looking for Althea Johnson. Does she reside here?"

The little girl looked up and hollered. "Althea! A peckerwood here to see you!"

Rowan craned his neck. His legs ached. *Four flights.*

Althea kept her apartment neat. The kitchenette was clean and there was a lovely fruit bowl on the otherwise bare dividing shelf. She explained that most of the apartments had upwards of ten people living in them, but she had been fortunate. "I bought into mine before this area was zoned for coloreds. I lived here before it was the black belt. Used to be a real nice place."

"When was that?"

"Oh, thirty-five years ago at least. It was before people drove cars."

The back end of Althea's voice was reedy and thin, but years of smoking had added a deep croak. Rowan thought it ideal for a storyteller. "From where did you move?"

"We came from Mississippi farms. Didn't know what to do in the city when we got here. Wasn't much prejudice when we came neither. Then the flood hit. Everybody and their mother came to Chicago. A few Negros are fine but thousands...That was too many black folks. It was even too many for me."

Rowan said, "I was in the Mississippi flood."

Althea's cheeks rose. "No shit? Was it as bad as they say?"

"Worse. I was in Vicksburg, working a case. The whole town was flooded over. I'll never forget the coffins."

"Coffins?"

"The ground had eroded, and the coffins from the cemeteries were unearthed. They floated through the town. It was the closest to hell I had ever seen—besides Chicago, of course."

"Of course. Chicago makes hell seem downright cozy. Was it a murder case?"

"Yes."

"Ooohhh, I love murder mysteries. Did you solve it in the library? Was it the butler who done it?"

"I solved it in the library, but it was not the butler. He was a very nice man named William."

"Congratulations. I'd make a terrible detective. I always get the killer wrong."

With a sudden skip of his heartbeat, he leaned forward in the chair. "It is not something of which I am proud. In fact, I now regret solving it."

Althea narrowed her eyes. "I ain't never heard of a detective regret solving a case. It don't sound right. That's their one purpose in life."

"It was a unique case. My client was a monstrous, evil man named Lasciva. He had murdered a woman and raped her daughter."

Althea's eyes bulged. "And he was your client? How does something like that happen?"

"It's a long story." The screeching chirps of cicadas swelled unbearably in the summer night. *Why now, Rowan? Why do you feel the need to confess this now?* "The daughter, Irene, came back and enacted her revenge."

"Did she poison him?"

He shook his head. "Decapitation."

"That'll do it every time."

"I turned Irene in to the authorities. She has been locked away in a Mississippi jail ever since—due to be released in three years and twenty-six days."

"Why on earth would you do something like that?"

Rowan hung his head. "Personal ethics, I suppose. The idea is if you extrapolate to the most extreme scenario and your behavior does not change, you will always know who you are. My personal ethics involve finding the truth and catching the criminal. As you said, it is my one purpose in life."

"Even if the criminal is the hero?"

"Yes."

"So, if you got this mumbo jumbo you call a code down pat, why do you regret catching her?"

"Because I would have killed the bastard had I been in her stead. He deserved to die."

"You sound a right mess in the head."

Rowan nodded. "An astute diagnosis."

"Life ain't that complicated." Althea sighed. "All right, Rowan. You wanted to come see me and I don't get many visitors 'cept the kind I don't want. What can I do you for?"

"I wanted to ask you about Clarence Williams." He pulled out a Camel.

Althea pointed at it with a bony, crooked finger. "Can I bum one of those?"

"Certainly, madam." He handed it to her.

"I ain't heard that name for a long time." She ran the paper-thin skin of her fingers along the cigarette. "Clarence was fun. He liked to dance. He liked to drink. Sometimes he liked to do other stuff. Not much else to say about him really."

Rowan lit her cigarette. "I like to drink."

"I would offer you something, but there's no alcohol. I can't afford it anymore."

He pulled out a five-dollar bill and put it on the table.

"Are you paying me to talk? I was already talking to you. You got the order of things all mixed up."

"No, I am offering to buy you a drink. Just being friendly." Rowan looked her over. "You have nice hair."

"It's a wig."

"Well, it is a lovely wig. Excellent...taste you have."

Her grin revealed yellow, acrylic dentures. "You ain't a real people person, are you? I can tell."

Williams would get a kick out of you. "Was Clarence your man?"

Althea exhaled smoke with a deliberate, thin breath. It reminded Rowan of steam spouting from a kettle. "I wouldn't call him that. Just a friend."

"Did he ever introduce you to any other women?"

She looked down at the bill. "How did you find me?"

"I went to the iron mill and talked with Andre."

"I'll be damned. How's Andre?"

"He has seen better days."

"Ain't we all? I loved his jaw." Althea's long fingers traced the outline of her jaw with mnemonic strokes.

"His jaw?"

"He had that Polack jaw. You ever seen a Polack's jaw? It's like a square. Plenty rugged. Ain't nothing like a strong man. After he's been working…chopping wood with the sawdust sticking to his skin. Mmm, mmm, mmm." Her body shifted in the chair from some other distant memory. "Sometimes Clarence would come by after work. Sometimes he'd bring Andre. He never brought any other women."

Rowan rubbed his bleary eyes. "Was Clarence a good man?"

"He was a happy man. Never held a grudge. Treated people nice. It's a shame what happened to him. The man couldn't swim and he ends up naked, drowned in a lake. Go figure."

"Do you know anyone who would have wanted him dead? Perhaps a jilted lover?"

Althea shook her head. "Clarence had plenty of those, but he was good to everybody. I know he put a few women in the family way. Always offered to pay to take care of it. Fellas don't do that nowadays. I heard he even got married once or twice."

"Do you remember any of the women's names?"

"I'm too old to remember names."

Rowan swallowed, feeling the solution drifting farther down the abyss of forgotten memories. "Do you at least know what happened to them? Did any of them remain in Chicago?"

"One woman was pregnant around when he died. I think she moved away."

"By any chance, was the woman involved in theater?"

"If she was, he never told me about it. Or maybe he did, and I wasn't listening. I didn't really have Clarence over for his conversation." She took a long drag and eyed him suspiciously. "Rowan?"

"Yes, Miss Johnson?"

"Smile."

At ten thirty the next morning, Rowan and Walter showed up for the postmortem report. Grady led them down to the lonely white-and-gray basement.

"Bombing's cleared up at least. The feds lost Thompson thanks to Young, but they got the union boss in custody. Guy named Heather. They think he was the mastermind behind the whole thing. After a week of turning the screws, he'll talk."

Rowan asked, "Can we talk to Heather?"

"That's a negative. The feds don't give a good goddamn about your case. I was lucky to get Grizz's razor from them. They also told me that my services are no longer needed. That means I am now on the Miller case, and you are to keep me informed of every move."

"Don't you mean the Pluviam case?" said Rowan.

"Either way, I'm after one guy, Manory, and his name is Timothy Brown. McKinley took one look at Grizz's razor and nixed it. The edge don't fit the throat. We bought the same razor that Brown uses and whatdya know? A perfect match." Grady nodded at Walter. "How's the mitt?"

Walter held up his bandaged hand. "My piano playing days are over."

"Didn't know you played."

"I don't. It's just something people say."

Grady narrowed his eyes. "Why the fuck would people say that if they don't play the piano? What sense would it make?"

Walter smiled dumbly at him. "You and Manory should really be working together. It'd be a laugh riot in that office. Nothing would ever get done."

"Have you gotten hold of Maura Lewis?" Rowan asked.

Grady stopped at the door to the morgue. "Maura Lewis was reported missing from the Oleanna Woman's Shelter up on Michigan and Thirtieth."

Rowan said, "A woman's shelter? Really?"

"Yeah. They keep tabs on their residents on account of all the missing people in the city. If the residents find housing, they are to notify the shelter or else they call the police. They called. One more thing." Grady pulled a card from his breast pocket. "I got your address in Baraboo. It's a Warners. I tried to call, but there's no phone."

Finally. "Outstanding. This case will be over in no time."

Grady tapped at Rowan's lapel. "You sure you're not holding out on me?"

"Grady, you have always been the third person to know what I know. I am working on the case. I will hand it to you with a bow. Trust me."

McKinley sat at the back table, smoking and playing solitaire. "We have to stop meeting like this, Manory."

Grady scowled. "She looks horrible. Couldn't you have put in some elbow grease or something?"

"Look what I had to work with," said McKinley, sweeping the cards into a deck.

Rowan said, "I imagine there were no surprises."

McKinley tossed his cigarette on the floor and squished it with his shoe. He joined them next to Allison's corpse. "The killer used a straight razor on the neck. He was right-handed, approached her from the front. There were two wounds to the neck. The first was quite shallow but just deep enough—a slashing motion from a relative distance. The second was a deep, oblique cut. I think he was standing over her body, used two hands to manage it. The slicing of the stomach and chest was done with a butcher knife, slightly jagged, at least six inches. After that, it's just chaos. Lots of gray wool fibers, so he was wearing gloves. He ripped out her organs with his hands. Sliced open everything. We aren't dealing with Jack the Ripper. This clown had no idea what he was doing."

Grady said, "Anything out of the ordinary?"

McKinley stared at him.

"Anything *else* out of the ordinary?"

"Standard disembowelment, as far as these things go."

"Would you say we're looking for a man?"

McKinley shrugged. "Not necessarily. Whoever did it had lots of time. There's so much hacking involved. I don't think our guy had to be strong. Might have been a woman. A determined one."

Rowan sighed. "All right, Grady. I will come back from Baraboo tomorrow evening and give you a full report."

"At least tell me what you expect to find."

"The Williams connection."

Walter looked at him.

Rowan shook his head. "Not you, the..." His eyes glinted. A smug smile came to his face. *That is what it was.*

Walter saw that look of astonishment on his boss's face. It had been a while since Walter had seen it. "I know that look."

Grady squinted. "What look? What are you two mugs talking about?"

"Nothing," said Rowan, pulling Walter along. "Nothing at all. Good day, Grady."

"Good day? Hey, no secrets, Manory. You know something, you tell me."

The detectives reached the main floor. Rowan nervously lit a cigarette in the corner. "Go back to the office. If the doctor from the hospital in New York calls, find out everything you can about the Pluviams. I'll call you later with instructions."

Walter asked, "Where are you headed?"

"Edward's house. Maura has moved up a notch on our suspect list."

"What makes you say that?"

"It was something that happened when I met the cast on the day of the opening. I noticed it, but I did not pay it proper attention. I think in my younger years, I would have picked up on it right away. Do you remember when you were talking to Maura in the dressing room?"

Walter pictured her Louise Brooks haircut. "Yeah. She said something about the killer being dangerous for everybody."

"Do you recall what she did?"

"No."

"I do. I could not fathom it at the time, but how could I have? I did not know then what I know now."

Maura looked at Edward's reflection in the mirror over the living room mantel. "Do you think one of us is next?"

"Nonsense. Timothy had a reason to kill Allison. He has no reason to kill us. You saw him on Tuesday; he was doped up on something. He wasn't himself."

"How did Allie die? Did she..." Maura sobbed. "Did she

suffer?"

"They wouldn't tell me. The cops just said she was murdered. I don't know why it hasn't been in the paper." Edward paused. "Did you catch up with Allie that night?"

"Obviously not. I ran after her, but I lost her."

"You left just after she did. How did you—"

"What's with the third degree? She went down an alley, and I fell down and lost her. Twisted my ankle real bad too."

"It looks fine now."

"It got better. Jeez Louise, Eddie, the police are after me. There's a killer out there. I'm scared." She put her palm over her forehead and let it slide down her face and onto her mouth.

"Why would the police be after you? Did you follow Allie to the theater? You can tell me the truth. I don't care if you did."

"What about you? Huh? Where did you go?"

"I came home, expecting to find you. But you weren't here. I haven't slept for the last two nights, been worried sick, and now you show up here and...Where have you been?"

She turned away from him. "Oh, Eddie, I'm sorry. You've been so good to me. I don't know who I can trust."

"It doesn't matter, Maura. I don't care why you're running from the police."

"Eddie, I—"

Edward tried to embrace her, but she flinched. "You don't think I'm the killer?"

"No, of course not."

"Then we'll leave, together."

"Where?"

"Who cares? We'll just go. Every time I read a murder mystery, I always wonder why the people don't just leave. I know you didn't do it, and you know I didn't either. We'll go tonight. Maybe out West."

"What about Christine?"

Edward looked up at the stairway. "I'll drop her off at the hospital. They have to take her in. I'll tell them she's not feeling well."

"Eddie?"

"I'd do it for you, Maura. I'll do anything for you. Whatever you've done, whatever you're running from, it doesn't change the way I feel about you."

A knock came at the door.

Edward pointed. "Upstairs. Go."

"It's the police? They'll come upstairs. They'll find me, Eddie."

"I won't let them. Go. Quickly."

Maura ran up the stairs, disappearing around the corner. Edward waited a few seconds and pulled the door open.

Rowan stood on the porch with flared nostrils. "Where is Maura Lewis?"

11

THE NASTY, DARK-HAIRED GIRL

12:12 p.m. Friday, April 12th

The long, mirrored mantel was lined with a precious collection of knickknacks Christine had collected over many years. Rowan put his index finger at the top of a miniature replica of the first Ferris wheel and spun it. "Tell me about the party, Edward?"

Edward relayed the primary events, leaving out some of the debauchery and coming to the point where Allison faced off with Timothy. "Allison said she knew how he had done it."

"How he had killed Lisa?"

"It wasn't crystal clear, but yeah, I think that's what she

meant. She said there was evidence, and she was going to bring to you." Edward's eyes grew wide. "That means the evidence was at the theater. It must have been why she went there."

"I am certain it is no longer in the theater. The killer has surely removed it."

"You mean Timothy?"

Rowan stared at him blankly.

"I don't want to believe he did it, but he knew she had evidence. He even told me he was going to kill her."

"Yes, and you knew she had evidence too, Edward."

"That's right I did. Everyone at the party heard her."

"Including Maura?"

"Yeah, but…" He seemed to mull over the idea for a moment but then rejected it. "No. No. That's…You're not…" The words eluded him. "It's ridiculous."

Rowan grabbed a chair from the fireplace and pulled it close to the table. "Where does Maura live, Edward? The police are having the damndest time finding the girl."

"I don't know where she lives. She never told me."

"That is difficult to believe. She was your date to the party. Obviously you and Maura have feelings for one another."

"We'd been planning to go to David Brouthers's party for a few weeks. She invited the cast so we could celebrate *The Balcony*. Since opening night, Maura and I have seen each other a lot, it's true, but we always meet somewhere. I've never picked her up at her house."

Rowan lit a Camel. It tasted of dust. "Are you in love with her?"

Edward raised his voice. "Yes, I am. I fell in love with Maura Lewis the moment I met her, it just took me a while to realize it. That's how I know she isn't the killer."

Rowan chuckled. "No, that is why you are blind to the possibility. The problem, Edward, is that there may not be a Maura Lewis. She lied about her address, she lied about where she was from, and I cannot imagine she has decided not to lie to you."

"Even if that's true, it doesn't make her a murderer."

"Have you ever heard of a man named Clarence Williams?"

"No, should I have?"

"I think Maura might be connected to this man. What's more, I think Maura might have had a reason to want Lisa dead because of him." He thought better of saying anything else. "Where do you think she is now?"

Edward shrugged. "I don't know."

"Would you tell me if you did?"

"Probably not. No, definitely not."

The top stair creaked, startling the men in the living room. Two thick, veiny legs hobbled down the stairs. Christine bunched up the hem of her white draping lace nightgown. Before each step, she paused several seconds and then firmly planted a foot. When she finally made it to the bottom, Edward was waiting to take her by the arm. "I don't know what it is about me and stairs."

He gently guided her to the corner chair next to the sofa. "I think it's impressive you can still get down by yourself. Christine, this is Detective Rowan Manory."

Rowan gave a slight bow. "Miss Filius. I'm a friend of your nephew's."

The sconce light cast a shadow over her face. "But you're almost my age. How could you be Eddie's friend?"

"I'm only forty-seven years old."

Christine squinted in the darkness. "You look a lot older."

"Thank you."

Edward rubbed her shoulders. "Were you able to sleep?"

"Much better." She gave Rowan a disapproving look. "Being sick is not fun. Especially when the end is so near."

Rowan sat back in his chair. He didn't particularly want to talk with this woman, but a few questions for Edward remained. "Are you ill, madam?"

"I spent three days in the hospital."

"Two days," Edward corrected her.

"I'm not crazy. Thursday I went in, all day Friday, and you picked me up on Saturday. That's three days."

Rowan gave a sympathetic look. "I am sorry to hear that. What was wrong with you?"

"I don't know. No one can give me a straight answer."

He looked to Edward.

"Last Thursday, she went into a brief coma."

Christine shook her head. "It wasn't a coma. A coma, you go to sleep. I could hear and see everything when it happened. I saw the look on Edward's face. The poor dear was so worried. And I saw that nasty girl."

The detective paused, a subtle gleam coming to his eyes. "What girl is that?"

Edward blurted out, "The nurse."

Rowan said, "The one with the bracelet? Nurse Gonzalez?"

"Yes, how did you know? Am I…am I under investigation?"

"Why were you fired, Edward?" asked Rowan.

Christine's face turned angry. "You've been fired? Oh, Edward. In this economy?"

"Yes, I'm sorry I didn't tell you. I wanted to wait until I found something else," Edward looked at Rowan, "so you wouldn't worry about me."

Rowan kept his gaze fixed. "Why were you fired, Edward?"

"For theft."

"What did you thieve?"

"Can we discuss this later?"

Christine said, "Edward, you don't need to steal. I'll buy you anything you need."

Rowan stayed on track. "What did you steal, Edward?"

Edward took a deep breath. "Morphine. I stole a bottle of morphine, and I sold it to some people at David Brouthers's party. I don't remember their names so don't ask."

Christine shook her head. "Kids these days. When I was his age, I wasn't worried about morphine. I certainly wasn't getting fired for stealing it."

Rowan gave a smug grin at Edward. "Really? *You* stole the morphine?"

"That's right."

Christine said, "You know I was his teacher in high school. He was a good boy then. Always did as he was told. Said *yes sir* and *yes maam*. Now he's selling drugs."

Rowan kept his eyes on Edward while he spoke to Christine. "What did you teach, Miss Filius?"

"I taught all ages and I taught every subject. Everything but mathematics. I could never understand it. Such a cold language."

Edward gave a tepid, nervous laugh. "Imagine how popular I was in school with my aunt as the—"

Christine's eyes lit up with the realization of a forgotten memory. She slapped at Edward's hand. "No, Eddie, it wasn't the nurse I saw." They both looked at her with astonishment. Rowan asked what she meant. "I didn't see the nurse. I saw the girl with the black hair."

Edward said, "She's tired."

Rowan took a long drag. "The girl with the black hair? She was at the hospital?"

Edward wrung his hands. "Christine gets batty sometimes, imagines things that aren't there."

Christine smiled. "She's the one whose voice I recognized. She's the reason I went to the hospital."

Edward tried to pull her from the chair. "Christine, it's time for you to go back to bed. You need to take longer naps. You get up too soon, and you're still half asleep. It isn't good for you."

She refused to budge. "I'm not tired though."

Rowan said, "What did she do to you, this black-haired, nasty girl?"

Edward said, "Mr. Manory, don't provoke her. You can't rely on what she says."

He kept his gaze on Christine. "What is the girl's name?"

"Christine, I'm taking you up to bed."

She tried to push Edward aside. "She wanted to kill me."

"Was her name Maura?"

Edward swung around and screamed, "Manory!"

The room remained quiet for a bit. Something far away was humming, but mostly the sound of stillness filled the air. *That is quite the temper you have there, Ed. I have not seen it before.* "May I use your telephone?"

Stunned, Edward only offered a meek nod.

Rowan tossed the unfinished cigarette into the fireplace and called the office. "Williams."

Walter sighed and put down the pencil. "I was just writing you a note, old man. I'd almost finished and now you call me and ruin the whole thing. What's the rumpus?"

"Drop everything. We need to find Maura Lewis immediately."

"No can do, boss."

"What do you mean, *no can do?*"

"I thought I'd take a little vacation."

"Where?"

"Adair."

"Adair?"

"I can rhyme with you if you've got time to spare."

"Timothy Brown's hometown? What do you hope to find …there…goddammit, stop it!"

Walter giggled. "I was looking at Grizz's map of Illinois, and Timothy's hometown was one of the circled cities. This plot might even be bigger than we thought. I figure while you're off in Baraboo, I'll head to Adair. It should take about nine hours, so it'll take me fifteen. Give me a couple days to report back. I'll either call you at the office when you get back, or I'll leave a message at the Brown Bear. This clue is calling me, Manory."

Rowan sighed into the telephone. "Have something good for me when you return."

"Will do. And hey, remember, as soon as we wrap this up, we're on a plane to Los Angeles."

"Yeah, yeah."

"Don't *yeah yeah* me. You promised me that—"

Rowan hung up. He put his hands on Edward's shoulders. "Do you remember when I told you about Lisa's fall?"

"Yes, you said it was like a trance."

"Or a coma. The same thing that happened to your aunt may have happened to Lisa Pluviam, only Lisa was not near a hospital, she was twenty feet in the air." He exhaled a long breath. "I know you have been lying to me."

"I—"

"Shut up. I know. Despite appearances to the contrary, I am not a fool. Was Maura alone with your aunt before she went into her coma?"

"Not really."

"Yes or no? The truth now."

Edward stammered. "Yes, but only for a few minutes."

"A few minutes may have been plenty of time. Has she offered to take care of Christine for you?"

He said nothing.

"Edward, Christine is in danger. I know you have feelings for Maura, but you've got to be careful. And for God's sake, don't leave her alone with your aunt."

Edward watched through the window as Rowan shuffled down the walkway to the street.

Christine said, "He's right. She'll try and kill you too, Edward. She pretends to be innocent. *Oh, I'm just a girl. I need your help.* Rubbish. She knows exactly what she's doing. Every moment, every single flip of the hair is calculated. I told you to get rid of her. You should have heard her in the attic. I've never heard such filth."

He made a break for the stairs, leaping two at a time up to the second floor. In the guest bedroom, the receiver lay off the hook. Edward stuck his head out the open window. The back gate to the alley was still swaying in the hot breeze.

12

RE-CAST

5:30 p.m. Friday, April 12th

Rowan tossed his suit coat over the desk. He felt the case had to be nearing its end. All the little gathered pieces had filled the outer edges of the puzzle nicely and at a reasonable pace. He would go to Baraboo the next morning, and the tangled web of revenge his mind had reconstructed would become altogether obvious. *It always reveals itself to be incredibly simple. Patience, old man.*

The phone rang. "Williams?"

The voice on the other end groaned. "No, ahh. This isn't Williams. Doctor Crandall."

"My deepest apologies. This is Rowan Manory Investigations.

How may I help you?"

"Are you Rowan Manory?"

"Yes, I am."

"Why doncha have a secretary? Mighty unprofessional."

"I will take it under advisement. How can I help you?"

"Well, ahh, like I said, I'm Doctor Crandall. I'm the chief of surgery at Mercy Hospital. I understand you've been trying to get a hold of me."

Rowan sat in his chair. "Yes, sir. Thank you so much for calling."

"About the Pluviam woman?"

"I take it this *is* the hospital she went to in 1913."

"Ahh, that's right. And there's been an accident?"

"A terrible accident, yes."

"Well, what happened?"

"Lisa was performing a scene at the top of a tower and, unfortunately, she fell twenty feet to her death."

"My God. Horrible news."

"Yes, there was a full house in the theater when it happened. It caused quite a bit of panic."

"I can imagine."

"I am attempting to contact her sister Jenny to inform her. Tell me, were you the surgeon who performed the amputation?"

"Uh-huh, ahh. I remember the Pluviams very well. Fine women. Such a shame about Lisa. Remarkably intelligent girl. Good looking too."

"Oh, I know."

"That's some real rotten luck she had. Probably the worst luck anybody's ever heard of."

"How do you mean?"

"Well, ahh, first she loses her hand. It turns out that doesn't stop her from becoming an actress—against all reasonable odds. Then what happens? She dies onstage in some sort of freak accident."

"No, I think you have misunderstood me. Lisa Pluviam is the one who died."

"Yeah, ahh. Lisa. The one who lost her hand."

"But..." Rowan dropped the phone. The gears in his brain began rolling forward. The puzzle flipped.

"Have you ever been here before?" The security guard pushed the button for the fourth floor.

"Never."

"Awful kippy. Awful kippy."

Rowan gave a polite smile and tried to think of the meaning of *kippy*. "How do you mean?"

With a rattling jolt, the elevator reached the fourth floor. The guard grabbed the handle. "Did you read the sign at the front desk?"

"I must have missed it."

"One hundred percent transparency."

There were eight rooms, four on either side. The walls to each room were glass, allowing everyone on the floor to see one another. Each room had an oblong desk with a client surrounded by anywhere from one to three skinny lawyers wearing double-breasted Livingston suits. The tie color appeared to be optional.

How witty.

Jenny Pluviam sat in the third room on the right, a small pile of papers and a mountain of pencils in front of her. She turned her head as Rowan came down the hall. He met her stare through the glass.

One of the lawyers frowned and shook his head. "Highly irregular."

The guard opened without knocking. "Terribly sorry, but there's an urgent message for Miss Pluviam."

The lawyer stood up and shook his fists. "No, no, no, Eli, we are discussing sensitive matters. This is highly irregular."

Rowan put his hands behind his back. "Miss Pluviam, this cannot wait. I regret to inform you that your younger sister, Jenny, has died. I hate to be the wicked messenger, but I thought you would like to know."

Jenny put her elbows on the table and clasped her stump. "Would you gentlemen give us a moment of privacy?"

"But, Miss Pluviam—"

"Fuck right off."

The suits collected the messy pile of papers without further comment. They scurried out the door and stood in the hall, staring in wonderment at the two poker-faced combatants in the room.

A maddening panorama of reflections bounced off one another at various angles on the glass. Several faded Rowans paced along with the real one. "They must spend a fortune on Windex."

Jenny began without Rowan prompting her. "There were two sisters long, long ago in the old, hard-up struggling days. She was always the clever one, the one who could write. I was the happy one. I loved people and parties. She preferred staying in and scribbling away at her precious stories. I'm not sure I can do our relationship justice in words, Mr. Manory, but we needed one another. She needed an object for her jealousy. When I came home reeking of alcohol with smudged lipstick and a smile on my face, she stewed with hatred, fed off of it like some monster in a fairy tale. I suppose I needed the stench of failure around me. I pitied her and it made me feel good to be able to pity such a helpless creature. It was some kind of love."

"You met Clarence?"

"Clarence is very important to you, but he didn't mean all that much to me. I wasn't in love with the man. He asked me to marry him. I refused."

"Was Jenny in love with him?

"Yes. When men have ignored you all your life, it must feel like true love when one drunkenly looks your way. One night, he came looking for me and Jenny answered the door and…let's just say that Clarence wasn't a very picky man. It was two months later when Jenny told me. I can see it like it was yesterday. She poured into the kitchen with this shit-eating grin. *I hate to be the bearer of bad news, but I'm pregnant and I'm getting married and you'll never guess the father.* The silly bitch thought it would devastate me. Wouldn't you know it, when she told him the news, he didn't serenade her with promises of his love. He offered to drive her to St. Louis for an abortion."

"Did she?"

"No, Jenny had the baby, a little girl."

"What happened to the child?"

"She went to an orphanage. Jenny wasn't interested in keeping a memento from her one night of bliss with Clarence."

"Did she kill him?"

"I always thought it was her."

"And you said nothing to the police."

She shook her head. "I told you. Clarence didn't mean very much to me. I was a little pissed when I had to make the trip to Baraboo, but I was also proud of my little sister."

Rowan sat down at the opposite end of the table. "Why?"

"She actually stood up for herself."

"No." He slammed his hand on the table. "*Why?*"

"Oh." She held up her right arm. "It didn't take long before I realized my acting days were over. There aren't many plays that call for a one-handed woman. I was lying in my hospital bed when she first mentioned the idea. We could both write. She would teach me. Now she pitied me, and she rather liked that. That's when it occurred to her, I'm sure of it. Things began to change for me. The first few months were hard. Children were the worst."

"Children?"

"On the street. Children have no filter. When they see my condition, they ask their mothers, *What's wrong with that woman? What happened to her?* People weren't as friendly as they once were, especially men. I began to stay away from everyone. I stayed inside, Mr. Manory. Ice cream and cigarettes became my best friends. Jenny changed too. She went outside more, quit smoking, got in shape. I called the school and asked if we could both get into the writing program. There were two spots held for us. One was for a playwright and one for an actress. That was it. One day, she dyed her hair black and she told me she could be me. I laughed it off, but Jenny wasn't joking."

"Why would you continue to dye your hair, keep up the charade? Even now, after returning to Chicago?"

"I don't expect you to understand. Have you ever read any Erik Erikson?"

Rowan slowly put it together. "Identity crisis. In the social jungle of human existence, there is no feeling of being alive without a sense of identity."

"That's right. Trouble was, I didn't have one anymore. I wasn't the woman I had been and there was no one else I could become. It wasn't even a conscious decision. One day she called me Jenny. I answered her. I've done it ever since. That's the one way I could live."

"So when your father died, you were the rightful heir. But your sister received the money."

She tossed back her blonde hair. "I threatened to reveal our secret if she didn't fund my play. I thought the death threat was a way for her to get back at me. Seems we'll never know now."

Rowan stood, his body shaking with contempt. "She chastised me for using too many words, said it was a habit from her writing days."

"She was a good writer, but she wasn't as good as I am. And she wasn't half the actress I was."

"Are you sorry she's dead?"

"I didn't want her to die."

"What if she wanted *you* dead?"

"Me? But…" Her mouth remained open, the lower lip wavering.

Now you see the obvious angle. "The biggest obstacle to murder is not the nerve, nor is it the inclination. No, no, it is the punishment. How does one get away with it? There are a million ways, most of them obviously transparent. One rather clever way is to paint yourself as the victim. Say, if you were to make it seem as if you are the one who is in danger. How to do that? Set it up properly."

"A death threat." Jenny's eyes softened.

"Yes. You receive the death threat. Then when the murder is committed, it can be called self-defense. That is all well and good, but the police—they will naturally wonder why you didn't report such a thing."

"You report it to a detective."

"No, not just any detective. You find a foolish, senile old…" Rowan's face curled in hateful knots. "Someone who was desperate enough to think that a beautiful woman would find him interesting. A man who would blind himself in an effort to believe. You tell him and then you beg him not to go to the police. Of course, he says yes. You have to be a good actress. You plan to tell him the scene upon which you found the note—the balcony scene. But this man, he's such a fool, he's the one who brings it up, and you sit back and ask, *Is that important?* He agrees to watch you. When your sister is called to the catwalk and thrown to her death, you say you witnessed her pointing a gun at you. You pay off Grizz a portion of your inheritance, and voila. Grizz is a hero. None of the audience members sees him do it because they are watching the actress on stage. Edward doesn't see it because the light on the catwalk is blinding from his position on the balcony."

"And the detective?"

"He confirms all the details. You give him a peck on the cheek and leave him comfortable in his ignorance."

"Well?" asked Jenny.

"Well what?"

"Is it better knowing the truth?"

"I do not know the truth. Tomorrow, I will take the train to Baraboo, and I will find out what exactly happened all those years ago." Rowan paused at the door. "In the meantime, you had better hope no one else discovers your identity."

"Why is that, detective?"

"Because if the killer wanted to murder Lisa Pluviam, then he has some unfinished business, doesn't he?"

13

EYEWITNESS

The last futile rays of the sun stretched to the flat Adair horizon, the streaky greens and purples melting into gray under the emergent moon. A row of traffic lined the road out to Peoria as the employees of Brown Laboratories steeled themselves for the ride home along lengthy, boring stretches of farms and muddy fields. At the opposite end of the town, the main street lay dormant, the families shutting themselves indoors for supper and gathering round the radio for an episode of Jungle Jim.

Brown Laboratories was isolated from the goings-on of Adair, only a few farms within a half-mile radius. People rarely drove by, and no one really knew what was done in the strange looking building besides what they read in the paper. From above, the construct resembled a *T* except the top short line was curved at the ends, as if someone had taken a hammer to the two top corners.

Walter came out of Dr. Brown's office with a rush of adrenaline he had not felt for some time. The receptionist poked her head out from behind her copy of *The Red House Mystery*. When Walter reached the desk, he froze. His eyes looked over the grain of the wood and lost focus.

She tilted down a thick pair of glasses with her pinky. "Are you all right, Mr. Williams?"

He sputtered to attention, and the focus came back. "Don't call me Mr. Williams. I'm not a school teacher. Call me Walter."

She chuckled, looking back at the door to Dr. Brown's office. "Are you all right, Walter? Did you find what you were looking for?"

"Oh, yes. I did, but I've remembered something just now. It didn't seem important before." *Lisa, Timothy, Edward, Allison, and Maura. The names!* The gears in his brain clicked into place, and the elusive puzzle revealed itself to him in all its complicated glory. "Oh, my God! Of course. Lisa—"

"It's Lucy."

"Lucy, I know who did it, and I think I know why. May I use the telephone?"

"Is it a local call?"

"How do you define local?"

"I'm not supposed to let anyone make calls, even the employees."

"It's terribly urgent. A matter of life and death."

Lucy rolled her eyes behind her glasses. "Really. People will die if you don't make your phone call?"

"I know it's a cliché, but it's the honest-to-God truth. Besides, a woman like you has to take pity on a man like me."

"Why is that?"

"Because I can see the wedding ring on your finger. That means my opportunity is over. I have to live with that tragedy for the rest of my life, and I'll forever curse that lucky son-of-a-bitch you call your husband."

"Jesus Christ." She twisted the phone and pushed it toward him. "Make it snappy."

Walter winked at her. He tried the office, but Rowan wasn't there. He searched his pockets and found the number for Dave Bowen at the Brown Bear.

"Yeah, Walter, we're kinda busy. What can I do you for?"

"Is Manory there?"

"Nah."

"I need you to give him a message when you see him. Can you do that for me, Dave?"

"Shoot."

"Tell him I solved the case. Well, a few things have to be checked out first, but I have the killer and method figured for sure. Tell him not to do anything, just wait for me. And make sure to hat I solved it before he did. Be real shitty about it, and rub

; face. If you have an evil laugh, this would be a good time
to use it."

"Walter, I've got a pencil that's about half an inch and the
back of a receipt. Give me a quick, succinct message."

"Walter solved it. You should have read the playbill.
California, here we come."

"Walter solved it. Shoulda read playbill. California. Okay,
Walt, I gotta go."

"Abyssinia." He grinned from ear to ear. "Enjoying the book,
Lucy?"

"I can't figure it out. The body is in a locked room, the brother
is nowhere to be found, it's impossible."

"Naw, it's easy. I went through practically the same thing
down in Mississippi, except when I did it, it was much more
complicated. And I had a flood to deal with."

"You solved a real locked-room mystery?" Her mouth fell
open like a drawbridge. "All by your lonesome?"

"That's right. I had help from my assistant, but he played a
very minor role. He mostly got in the way."

She pointed to his bandage. "What happened to your hand?"

"Communist."

"Wow, you must live an exciting life."

"Not compared to Adair." He gave two knocks on her desk.
"Thank you, Lucy."

"Anytime, Walter."

A solitary bulb provided the only source of light outside the building. Walter walked to the parking lot behind the laboratory, his shoes trudging through the mud and onto the pavement. He scraped his feet and got into the car.

Manory will be happy. It's always the smallest detail that gets the noggin joggin. No more opening night murders. He heard it, plain as day. His brain really is getting old. The Manory from ten years back would have solved this case four days ago in his office. Los Angeles will fix him right up. The beach and the sunshine must do wonders for the mind. It would do wonders for Lucy, too. Poor girl. Gotta work in this building all night. Fumbling with a flashlight and a map, he planned his route back to Chicago as he whistled. *There she is. There she is. That's what keeps me up at night. Oh Gee whiz, Oh Gee whiz. That's why I can't eat a bite. Now ain't she sweet? See her coming down the street. I ask you confidentially, ain't she...*

Baraboo Station was a glorified log cabin with foliage growing spastically around the sides. A gangly old man with a pipe and a farmer's hat bent down to the window pass. The pipe clacked against his false teeth as he spoke. "What are you looking for?"

Rowan yelled through the glass. "It is a general store named *Warner's!*"

"This is Baraboo. I don't know where you think you are."

Rowan yelled louder. "Warner's!"

The man straightened his head to think about it and then bent back down, pulling the pipe from his mouth. "Do you mean, Warner's?"

"Yes!"

After a ten-minute walk and a short conversation with the manager, Rowan was directed to the back exit. A small pond and a rather unkempt garden of coexisting dead and living flowers sat next to an abandoned junkyard, the scraps of metal rusted and far past any useful condition. The whole area was engulfed in wild stalks of weeds and dirty crabgrass. A small girl stood knee deep in the water, splashing it idiotically with her arms. An aging woman with a taut face and tense jaws watched her from a lawn chair, a cigarette and an iced tea occupying her hands. Rowan cautiously approached her, the yearbook tucked under his arm.

"Mrs. Ber?"

She cocked her head. "Yes?"

"Thank goodness. I was worried you were no longer employed here."

"I'm retired. My grandson runs the place now. That little angel is my granddaughter, Edna."

Rowan half-heartedly nodded toward the pond. "Lovely child."

"Little Edna must be supervised constantly. While my grandson works, I watch Edna. Edna suffers from Pica. Are you familiar with Pica, Mister…?"

"Manory. No, I'm not."

She set the drink down, slapped the ants off her knees, and

approached him. "Well Mr. Manory. It's a disease you don't want to have. I can assure you of that."

As opposed to other diseases? "Mrs. Ber—"

"She has a compulsion to swallow things."

"I believe we all have the compulsion to swallow things." He patted his gut. "Some of us more than others."

"Things, Mr. Manory. Things."

"What sort of things?"

"Mostly metal things. Screws, nails, things like that. I can't watch her all the time. She doesn't even know she's doing it. There must be about a pound of metal inside her. God only knows what else she's stuffed in her gullet over the years."

"I seriously doubt it comes to a pound. She would not be alive."

"Oh, Edna's time isn't long. If she swallows one more thing, her stomach might not hold out. That's why I put her in the pond. Everything's natural in that pond. If she eats plants or bugs, or...I don't know. What else is in a pond?"

"Protozoa. Bacteria."

"Let her eat bacteria. It's better than metal."

"I'm sure it is. I don't mean to be rude, but I've traveled a long way to find you, Mrs. Ber."

"I can't imagine why. I'm a nobody."

"In 1912, a man was murdered up in Devil's Lake."

"Clarence Williams."

Rowan stood back, stunned. "You remember him?"

"I've never forgotten his name, the poor man. But, they didn't know for sure that he was murdered."

"He drowned."

"He didn't know how to swim. Of course he's gonna drown. That's just common sense."

"Why would he drive from Chicago to go swimming, if he did not know how to swim? Why was his car found back in Illinois?"

"I think about it every so often, I do. What if he drowned and that poor woman I saw him with, she panics? Right? She drives away and it isn't her fault. Besides, people have been known to do stupid things. They are *people* after all."

"The police brought a suspect here."

"If that's what you'd call her."

"You refused to identify her."

"I couldn't identify her. She had dark hair and she was skinny."

"And the woman you saw all those years ago with Clarence Williams was fat and had blonde hair."

"The word I used was pudgy. She wasn't fat. I couldn't call her fat. That would be overstatement."

"Mrs. Ber, would you remember the woman's face if you saw it now?"

"Of course."

"You are certain?"

"It's one of those moments in my life that plays in my head every so often. Comes at the darndest times, too. I'll be peeling carrots, and I'll see her face. I know exactly what she looks like or at least, what she looked like then."

"Good." He opened the book and held it in front of her. "Do you see that woman in any of these photographs?"

She looked down, her eyes scanning the page again and again, until they finally settled. Her lips parted open. "Oh, my God."

"You see her, don't you?"

She pointed. "That's her."

Rowan looked down at the photo under her finger. His face went slack.

"As sure as we're in Baraboo, that's the woman I saw."

Mrs. Ber was not pointing at either of the Pluviams, nor any other student on the page. Her finger was pointed at the top row of teachers. She was pointing at Christine Filius.

14

DOCTOR BROWN

Officer Young adjusted the rearview mirror. "Grady told me I'm to drop you off in Adair and then stay to make sure you can drive your partner's car back."

Rowan said nothing.

"I said I'm responsible for getting you back to Chicago."

"You may leave as soon as you drop me off. I will have no need for you then."

"I'm sorry about what happened. Walt was a good guy. It's got to be rough. I hope they catch the bastard who did it."

"I will catch him."

"You should get to sleep. It's about two more hours and

you're going to be exhausted when we get there."

"In which direction are we headed?" asked Rowan.

"To Adair."

"I mean on a compass."

Young thought for a second. "Southwest."

Oh, Walter.

The sheriff slid his glasses into his shirt pocket. "I understand you were friends with the deceased."

Rowan's voice cracked a bit, so he lowered it. "Yes, to tell the truth, my only friend." His bottom lip stuttered up and down. He was terrified he was going to cry.

The sheriff lowered his head, "I know this'll be hard for you. So, I thought we'd go in there together, and I could lead us in prayer? Was Walter a God-fearing man?"

Rowan nodded politely. "He was Baptist."

"Here in Adair, we're mostly Methodist. I don't think that'll make a bit of difference though. It don't matter the sect."

Walter's pale corpse lay atop a white sheet on a patient bed. The slash at the throat began as a high curve on the left side and then followed a slight dip as it traveled to the right.

"In your hands, oh Lord, we humbly entrust our brother, Walter Williams. In his life you embraced him with love. Deliver him now from every evil and bid him eternal rest where there will be no sorrow, no weeping or pain, but fullness of peace and joy with your son and the Holy Spirit. Amen."

"Amen." *Blood under one cracked nail. The bandage completely bloody from grasping at the throat, the other just under the nail, chipped on the dash. It was from the backseat.* "Where was the car found?"

"On Main Street. It's a small strip, about two blocks. He was parked in front of the mechanic's. I think Walter was killed while sitting in the front seat and then dragged into the back."

"Any witnesses? Anyone see another car? Perhaps a blue Auburn sedan?"

"This town only has two hundred and thirty people. No one sits around Main Street after dark, everything's closed. Would you like to go have a look at the car?"

"In due time." He fumbled for a cigarette. "I will arrange for the body to be driven to Chicago in the morning. Right now, I need to find Dr. Edmund Brown."

"That's easy. Doc Brown will be at the laboratory."

Rowan checked his pocket watch. "At this hour?"

"He works overnight with his secretary. Do you think he had anything to do with the murder?"

"Not directly. Also, if you would be so kind, I'd like a list of theaters near here. Perhaps a fifty-mile range."

"That might take a bit of time."

"Whenever you can. I will call you in the next few days."

"I'll do my best. Well, I'll wait outside and give you a moment alone."

Rowan took a drag. "Why?"

The sheriff played with the brim of his hat. "I think you should say something to him. How long did you two fellas know each other?"

Rowan froze. "Fifteen...no, sixteen years. We met at the annual Policeman's Ball. I was in the corner nursing a drink and praying no one would talk with me. Of course, he walked right up and introduced himself. Williams could talk with anyone. He had that gift. He enjoyed people." He turned to the corpse. Walter's face was pained, the shock carved into the cheeks. "I was thinking in the car ride here, what my last words to you were. I could not recall. I know I hung up the phone on you." The last word choked in his throat. He pinched the bridge of his nose, desperately holding on to his composure. "Do not worry, my friend. You may rest easy now. I will catch him." He bent down and kissed Walter's forehead and stroked back his brown hair. "He will pay for this."

Doctor Brown's lips rubbed against each other when he wasn't speaking. A rhythmic sort of tic, it came across as wholly unnatural. "I reckon I remember Mr. Williams. It were only two nights ago. Ain't that old yet."

"I need to know exactly what he asked you and what you told him."

"Now looky here, Mr. Williams done give me assurance no more trouble was coming my way. It's not two days later, and another detective is here asking me questions. What good's anyone's word if it gets broken so quick?"

"If my friend made such an assurance to you, then I am certain the assurance will stand."

He tapped a shaking finger on the page of an open tome. "Then what are you doing here? What did this Williams fella tell you?"

"Mr. Williams told me nothing. He was found on Main Street Sunday morning with his throat slit. You were one of the last people he spoke with, and you will tell me what it was you spoke about. Currently, I would prefer to keep the police out of this, but if you give me no choice, I will break Mr. Williams's word, and in two days time, some extremely clumsy, accident-prone Chicago cops will search your building, and they will find something incriminating whether it is here or not."

"Good Lord! I..." Brown stood up and walked to a propped globe in the corner of the room. He slapped at it, spinning it around a few times. "Well, this is a right mess, ain't it now?"

"What did you and my friend discuss?"

"I asked him what he was doing here. Then he asked me what I thought he was doing here. I told him he was probably here on account of my son."

"Timothy."

Brown nodded. "I've made mistakes in my life. Show me one man that didn't. None have cost more than my boy. It's too late now."

"What did Timothy do?"

"The pyrotol."

Rowan lit a cigarette. "What pyrotol?"

"It's a—"

"I know what it is."

"I keep it at my farm. When the government sold off the last batches, I stockpiled it."

"Timothy stole it."

"Some of it, aye. There was that explosion up in Chicago and I read that they used pyrotol. I didn't think too much of it at first. It ain't gold for Christ's sake."

"Keeping this information to yourself is a serious offense."

"Walk a mile in my shoes. Wouldn't you protect your boy? He was always different, Tim. Aimless with idle hands. You know what they say about idle hands?"

"Do you know Timothy's current location?"

"Yeah. He's at his sister's, 1422 Montrose. The house is in her husband's name. They went to France for the summer. He called me from there. The boy is scared, Mr. Manory. I think he's done strung out on something."

"Is Timothy a communist?"

Doctor Brown sputtered with indignation. "Ridiculous. Timmy's too stupid to have views. If it were political, then he musta been coerced."

"What else did Williams ask you?"

"We talked about how awful Chicago was. He said he was going to California. He was sure of it now."

"When did he say that?"

"I reckon it was right before he left."

"And what were you talking about just before."

"I told you—"

"Specifically, what were you discussing the moment before he was sure about going to California?"

"Well, Mr. Williams was a big talker. Talked a whole bunch. Uhh…I told him that this was just offices and laboratories and the plant proper is in Glenview."

"And?"

"And that Glenview ships medical supplies to hospitals in Chicago."

"And?"

"And we recently sent a new drug for testing. Curare."

Rowan took a long satisfying drag of smoke. "That is…How would you call it?"

"A powerful muscle relaxant. You find it in South America. The natives use it to hunt black buck and wild boar. It's been around for a long time. In the 1840's, civilized people discovered it. We've been experimenting and, it's just about done ready. I reckon five years before we can use it on patients." He chuckled. "Another fine example of how the empirical knowledge of them backasswards rainforest Indian tribes can be made useful by Western science and the pharmaceutical industry."

"Curare is mentioned in a few stories of Sherlock Holmes. How does it function precisely?"

"It acts upon the voluntary muscles 'stead of the nerves or

heart. The subject feels everything that's happening, but can't move. It's completely safe, except you need artificial respiration. I told that sumbitch up at Garfield to get himself an iron lung before I'd think about sending it to him. What was his name?"

"Okay, okay." Rowan rubbed his face. "Can it be ingested?"

"That would make it awful for hunting. No, there ain't no effect when you swallow it."

"Absorbed by the skin?"

"Nuh-uh."

"It must be injected?"

"Yup."

"That does not help. I have a woman who..." He raised his head. "Does it matter where it is injected?"

"As long as it comes in contact with capillaries. Cases have been reported of blow darts landing on the meat-paw of a boar and still workin' their effect. Depending on where it enters the body, it might take more time. If you inject it directly into the bloodstream, we're talking five minutes. Once...What the hell's wrong with you?"

Rowan was standing now. "How long would the effect take if the curare were introduced into capillaries rather than the bloodstream?"

"Thirty minutes. Maybe forty."

"How is curare detected?"

"We ain't found a way yet. It goes from the blood to the tissue and then vanishes, plum undetectable."

Rowan's heart raced in his chest. His limbs felt light and he thought he might faint. "How much is needed?"

"Less than a thimble. Now look here detective—"

"Is there a factory involved in the production of needles in Glenview?"

"Ya'll mean a needle plant?"

"Is there?"

"Yes sir, John James. We bought it out last year."

"Thank you, Doctor Brown."

"Now looky here, my boy ain't bad, just confused."

"I am not interested in your boy."

The puzzle pieces had been forced into the wrong places. Now the frayed, interlocking edges fit uneasily together in front of him. Perhaps they would—

"Hey."

Rowan stopped at the front door and looked back to the desk.

The woman peeked out from the last few pages of her novel. "Are you a friend of Walter's?"

"I am."

"Tell him that if he ever finds himself back in Adair, he needs to make sure to stop in and say hi to Lucy."

15

AND THEN THERE WERE TWO

12:02 p.m. Wednesday, April 18th

Rowan lurched into The Brown Bear and sidled to the bar. His reflection in the mirror was unrecognizable. The details were all there—mustache, fat gloomy cheeks, broad nose—but the gleam, that telltale gleam of life that flashes from the eyes, was absent.

Dave wiped the bar clean. "You know, Manory, it's not my job to tell a paying customer that they have a problem. Hell, that would be awful for my business."

"I need you to do something for me, Dave. Will you help me?"

"Sure. You name it."

"Can you call down to the precinct and read this message to

the desk man?"

Dave took the sheet of paper from his hands. He looked it over. "You want me to read this?"

"If you would be so kind."

"Can I ask you one question?"

Rowan nodded.

"Why don't you tell them yourself?"

"Because they might recognize the sound of my voice."

"And why—"

"You're about to ask a second question, Dave. I only agreed to answer one."

"When you're right, you're right." Dave dialed the station. He spoke in a falsetto. "Hello, this is…Tina. You need to go to 1422 Montrose. Timothy Brown is upstairs in the bed, dead of an apparent morphine overdose. Lying next to him, you will find the same razor used to kill Allison Miller. I shall call you soon with further instructions. Um…have a nice day."

"Thank you, Dave."

"Are you still working on the case of the lady that fell?"

"Yes. Only two suspects remain; the list has been narrowed down, Chicago style."

"And both of them could have done it?"

"Yes. They both had the opportunity. All I need is one more clue. I'm sure of it."

"You think you'll find that clue here?"

"No. I think I will find a glass of scotch here, and I could use a drink. Also some cigarettes."

"You don't smoke pre-rolled."

"I do now." His fingers rattled softly on the bar.

"I got something for you to try. Glendronach. The Czechs and the Germans know beer, but the Scots know whiskey."

"What are you, Dave?"

"I'm Irish."

"And what do you know?"

"I know how to marry the wrong gal and ruin my life."

For the first time in days, a smile appeared on Rowan's face. He held up the glass and through the ruddy liquid, saw a familiar image on Dave's wall. The creases of the smile ironed out.

Dave turned around to see what Manory was staring at. "The flyers?"

Rowan pointed. "That one."

Dave pulled it off the wall and placed it on the bar. "Maureen? Do you know her?"

"I do. Williams knew her too."

"Oh yeah, did you talk with Walter?"

"About what?"

"He called here with a message for you. He said he solved the case."

Rowan blinked. "Williams solved it?"

"Let me find that receipt."

Rowan downed his whiskey. His fists scrunched the sides of the flyer.

Dave pulled it out from the register. "Here it is. 'Walter solved it. You should have read the playbill. California here we come.' That mean anything to you?"

Rowan fumbled through the pockets of his suit coat and pulled out the tobacco-crusted, folded playbill. He read it twice before the look of astonishment came to his face. He looked back at the flyer.

Dave polished a glass. "You're not gonna like California. Everyone's pretty over there. They ain't ugly like you and me."

"What have you got behind the bar, Dave?"

"My insulin and some Benzedrine. I don't touch the hard stuff."

"No, Dave. What have you got behind the bar?"

Dave paused. "A twenty-two. Why? I don't like the way you look, Manory. You're lookin' feral."

The alley behind Taylor fell under darkness. A mild rain drizzled through the gray, hazy sky. By the time Rowan reached the back gate of Edward Filius's home it was pouring down harder and faster with swirling winds. The pavement under his feet turned black and slick. Water dripped off the sides of his face, blurring his vision. An earthy stench of Petrichor emanated from the wet neighborhood lawns. He poked his fingers through the chain link.

A walkway lay next to the house, extending from the gate to the front sidewalk. The bent, barren clothesline swayed over patches of muddy brown grass. All the curtains to the windows were drawn.

The metal made a tiny trill when Rowan flipped the latch, causing the hairs on the nape of his neck to rise with anticipation. The slow, steady croaking of the gate matched the tight rumbling in his gut. With one stolid step at a time, he marched toward the house.

He was nearly past the back yard when Maura Lewis came up the opposite side of the walkway. Her eyes were staring straight at the ground, looking out for the unlucky cracks and puddles. Rowan's heart gave out an arrhythmic beat as he slid Dave Bowen's twenty-two out of his suit pocket and waited.

Maura reached the house and, at the last possible moment, noticed Rowan at the fuzzy edges of her vision. The rain cascaded off the gutters and splashed on the pavement between them.

Rowan licked his lips and drew back the corners of his mouth. "Maureen Williams!"

16

CURTAIN

1:15 p.m. Tuesday, April 17th

She ran as fast as she could, cutting straight through the neighbor's lawn out to the street. Rowan jogged a few meaningless steps but quickly lost his balance, flopping onto the concrete. The gun skidded along the walkway, splashing in the middle of a puddle. He rolled over into the mud, trying desperately to get his footing. Maura was gone. In those few seconds, the girl was gone.

The Chicago rain turned merciless, pelting him like a storm in a jungle. The flesh on his stomach and hands turned raw from scraping the concrete. Tiny cracks of blood seeped wet pink stains into his shirt. He thought he might sit there forever, wallowing in misery with his muscles easing into stillness and never moving again. But no...*You have to catch her.* Rowan pushed himself from the ground, pocketed the gun, and staggered around to the front porch.

The howling wind took hold of the door when Edward opened it. "Detective? What's happened? You look awful."

"I know. I am so sorry, Edward. I...May I use your phone one more time?"

"Do you need a doctor?"

"Only the telephone." Rowan spread a filthy trail of mud across the wood floor while Edward struggled to pull the door shut. His hands shook as he dialed the station. "Grady."

"Manory. Good God, where are you? You need to get down to 1422 Montrose."

"Grady, Maura Lewis is running down Taylor toward Schiff. Send everyone you can after her."

"Fine, but we found Tim Brown. He's—"

"Maura's your priority now. You cannot let her escape." Rowan hung up the phone and leaned over the back of the chair until he heard something crack. "Oh God, I am tired, Edward."

"You found Maura?"

"She will be taken in soon enough. The girl cannot hide forever."

Edward shook his head with disapproval. "It's not Maura. Whatever you're thinking, whatever scheme you've got in your head, it's wrong. Timothy is—"

"Dead."

His voice quieted. "Tim's dead?" Edward fell onto the arm of the sofa. It was as if all the air had been released from his body. "Oh, no."

"Overdose. Whether accidental or intentional, I do not know. I discovered his body this morning along with both of the murder weapons."

"Both?"

Rowan dug into his pocket and tossed Edward one of Lisa's earrings. "Give the post a twist," he said, twiddling his fingers in the air.

Edward did as instructed. The post pulled free from the hollow, smoky glass ball.

"Do you know what curare is, Edward?"

"Not really. I know it's a chemical. I delivered a shipment to the hospital."

"That's right, you did. It was on the day before opening night, I believe." Rowan took a quick look out the window, checking if Maura was lurking outside. "Do you know what it does?"

As Rowan explained the effects of curare, Edward ran his nail down the post, finding the tiny groove of the hole. "Yeah, but how would this earring work?"

"It is quite simple. The post is much like the needle on a bicycle pump. Of course, the dimensions would be an issue. It had to match the gauge of Lisa's earrings. To solve this dilemma, the post was made at the John James needle plant in Glenview. The end of one needle was pressed into the beginning of another and then filed down to the proper size. The glass pearl was made at Eisenberg's Jewelry. I found their business card in Tim's wallet. They make theatrical jewelry. In fact, they made Lisa's real earrings for the play. It was quite the appropriate finale for an actress, don't you think? Killed by artifice."

Edward squeezed the earring in a fist before setting it on the coffee table. "Let me tell you about Maura Lewis, because you seem to have the wrong idea about her."

"I've never met Maura Lewis." He pulled out a Camel with his teeth.

"Maura is childlike. She keeps a diary. She makes silly jokes. We were at Danny's Restaurant last week, and she...she...she played peek-a-boo with a baby at another table." He pointed at the earring. "You're telling me she's an evil genius who could plot something like this. I can't believe it."

"Oh, Edward, I know a sap when I see one. Believe me, I do. There's one staring back at me in the mirror every morning. Maura's a very good actress, a pretty good storyteller too. Right about now, I am supposed to think that this case is wrapped up. That was her plan anyway. Now, I can finally see the whole puzzle. Maura will be captured soon and brought to justice. While we wait, I will explain it to you. Forgive me if I ramble a bit; it will be the first time I say all this out loud."

Edward threw his arms in the air. "You can try."

"Lisa Pluviam had a plan—a rather clever one—to kill her

sister." He took a drag. "God, they taste awful. Grizz agreed to kill Jenny Pluviam in exchange for two things: a portion of her inheritance and some pyrotol. Do you know what that is?"

Edward nodded. "I read about it in the newspaper. It was used in the bombing."

Rowan's eyes widened. "Yes, they waited to release that information in the newspapers. That detail plays a small role in the story. But I won't get ahead of myself just yet. God knows it's easy to lose yourself in the dizzying details. Grizz received the pyrotol from Lisa, but he was unable to collect the money for reasons that are now quite obvious. The wrong Pluviam died. More importantly, Grizz was identified as being near the location of the bombing. This unfortunate turn of events sent him into hiding. But this plot, which I wasted so much time on, is neither here nor there; it is essentially a red herring. Let us drop Grizz for the moment and focus our attention on Lisa." He paced as he spoke, the pink stain spreading across the gut of his untucked shirt. "The weekend before the play, Lisa accompanied Timothy to Adair. That's how she obtained the pyrotol. After that, she had no more use for him. With the incendiary material in a suitcase and the, shall we call it, carnal pleasures had, Lisa ended their tryst."

"Did Timothy make the death threat?"

"Keep up, Edward. The death threat is not important. It never was." A lightning bolt flashed somewhere far off in the dark gray sky. Trees bent over backwards, the sound of their rustling branches filtered into the room softly, offering only hints of outdoor fury. "You are an actor. You concern yourself with plots. Let us examine the plot Maura so desperately wants me to believe. She would like me to think Timothy was so heartbroken, he decided to kill Lisa. I freely admit some of the Timothy theory fits. He had access to curare because his father is developing it for use in surgical procedures, and Timothy could have easily had the posts made in Glenview. The earrings are studs, which would allow for a natural, rather smooth flow through the post. Tim knew that Lisa bled whenever she wore earrings. It took longer than usual for the curare to take effect because of the placement, but the ear has capillaries. The liquid would be absorbed rather lazily by the infected, bleeding lobes. Less than a thimble of curare is necessary, say half a thimble in each ball. The glass is clouded which hides any of the contents therein. It was a wonderful plan, but it was not Timothy's."

Edward's breath grew heavy. The rain formed cascading waterfalls over the windows. "Oh gosh, Maura's out there all alone. Did you...did you at least go to Eisenberg's and ask them who paid for the jewelry?"

"When I visited Eisenberg's this morning, they told me that Timothy had asked them to make the earrings, yes."

He slapped his knee then pointed at Rowan. "There you are. How is that not proof?"

"Just a few more minutes, and everything will be clear. So, let us say that Timothy had planned this perfect murder. What went wrong? There was the communist plot and the note which drew some unfortunate attention. And of course, me—I would be in attendance. If Lisa were to die, murder would have to be suspected. Timothy was scared. Remember what he said? *Cancel the play.* When I interviewed him afterward, he did not want me to know Lisa had rejected him because he would be a prime suspect. When women are left by men, they sometimes weep, but when they *leave* men, they are sometimes murdered. The mechanics of his plan worked. Lisa died, and I had no clue how it was done. Unfortunately for Timothy, Allison ruined everything. After he switched the curare-loaded earrings, Timothy had to get rid of the originals. If the police searched him and found a pair of Lisa's earrings, it would raise suspicion. So, he hid them in the chest of drawers. Not very bright, but it was done in the face of panic. Plus, there was lots of jewelry in the dresser to camouflage their presence. Somehow, Allison found them."

Edward's mouth gaped. "That's why she came out to the crossover. She had them in her hand to give them to Lisa. And then—"

"And then she was gobsmacked." A crack of thunder boomed so loud that it shook the foundation of the house. "Lisa was already wearing the earrings. Now, obviously Allison couldn't have realized exactly what was happening, but after Lisa's mysterious death, she knew something was afoot. Allison opted to keep quiet—told the police nothing. They had nothing on her besides the hastily made threat. Why would she talk? This brings us to the fascinating journey of the earrings themselves. You accidently stepped on one of them, but the other remained attached to the ear of the corpse." He paused. *All you need to be an actor is a set of ears.*

"What is it?"

"Nothing. Where was I...? Oh yes, the earring. It ended up in the morgue and was eventually delivered, along with Lisa's clothing, to Jenny, who promptly threw it in the trash. Allison, intrigued by this mysterious extra jewelry, collected it. I noticed the garbage can was turned over when I visited Jenny, but I thought it was the work of the neighborhood raccoons. They frequent those wide-open fields next to her house."

Edward nodded, following the detective's story. "Then she saw how the earring worked. How did she know it was this...how do you call it?"

"Curare. She didn't, but I imagine she knew it must have been some kind of poison. Then came the party. Allison foolishly revealed she was in possession of the evidence. Tim followed and killed her with his razor. He now had the proof, but committing murder is a lot like lying; one time rarely suffices. You must do it again and again, continuing to cover the various, newly formed tracks until the web you have weaved is so dense it catches your throat and strangles you. My friend..." Rowan choked on the words. "My friend Walter was found killed in Adair on Saturday. I am sure the razor that was used belonged to Timothy."

Edward meekly clasped his hands together in his lap. "I'm sorry. I didn't know him well, but he seemed like a good man."

"The best." Rowan sniffled and cleared his throat. "Then Timothy returned to Chicago, where, racked by guilt, he soothed himself in the pleasures of morphine. He is found with the earrings and his razor conveniently by his side. That is the plot I am meant to believe. What about you, Edward? Do you believe that plot?"

Edward's voice faltered. "I guess so. Timothy is a much more plausible killer than Maura."

"But that is preposterous."

"Why?"

"Oh, let me count the ways. Timothy and Lisa went to Adair a week before the play. She ended the relationship on Sunday. I am to believe that he planned her murder from Monday to Thursday, a meager four days! The woman at Eisenberg's workshop informed me Timothy ordered the earrings during the third week of March. Are you telling me he had them made just in case Lisa would rebuff him later? And we don't really need evidence, do we? This was a work of genius. That would be quite the generous adjective for Timothy Brown. Besides, the man who plans a perfect murder kills Allison with his own razor? No. How did he know Williams was on his way to Adair?"

"Wouldn't he start taking morphine because he felt guilty and wanted to escape?"

"Oh, guilt was the reason he turned to drugs, but not because of these murders. When it was finally revealed in the newspaper that pyrotol had been employed to kill those innocent people at the Federal Building, Timothy realized how Lisa had used him and he had, however unwittingly, been involved in the murder of eight innocent people."

Edward remembered. *"One of them in a goddamned stroller. That's what he meant at the party when he asked me what one more dead body would matter."*

"Timothy was sensitive. Most people couldn't see that, but it was obvious to me. He cried for Lisa. He wanted to protect her whether she loved him or not. The man was so distraught over the threat to Lisa's life he could barely remember his lines. No, it was not Timothy that killed Lisa or Allison...or Walter. All he did was purchase some earrings—for a friend."

Edward's eyes became glossy. "But it...it wasn't Maura."

Rowan smiled. "There was one other thing I learned at the jewelry shop. Timothy told them for whom the earrings were made. He told them the earrings were a gift for Maura Lewis."

"He told them that?"

"Do you remember when we first met, Edward? It was in the dressing room. I was giving my speech to the cast about the death threat. At one point, I called out Williams's name. Do you remember what Maura did?"

An empty, fluttery feeling took over Edward's stomach. He cried helplessly. "But Maura..."

Rowan ignored him. "It was a small detail, seemingly unimportant at the time. When I said *Williams*, she looked at me. I thought she had recognized me. But it was not recognition. There was something automatic in her response. It was as if the girl were responding to her own name."

Edward wiped his eyes with his knuckles. "So, her name is Maura Williams? So what?"

"Today, I saw a very interesting photograph. It was on a flyer for a missing person. One *Maureen* Williams, a pretty girl with buck teeth and freckles. She's been missing for a while now." An inch-long piece of ash hung from his Camel. "Let us try a different plot, one that makes a bit more sense. Just to see if it works. Long ago, a little after Maureen was conceived in fact, a man named Clarence Williams went to Devil's Lake with a woman."

"What happened at Devil's Lake?"

"Excellent question, Edward. No one really knows. Clarence was found in the lake, drowned. Murder was suspected, and Lisa Pluviam was the primary suspect. Alas, the police could not tie her to the crime. Most people who knew Lisa assumed she had done it, though. You see, Clarence was romantically linked with Lisa, and he had impregnated her sister, Jenny." Rowan flicked the miniature Ferris wheel. "This Clarence Williams was a bit of a cad, had many girlfriends. He even married one woman, impregnated her too. According to the information on the flyer, Maureen's mother now lives in Burlington. It's about twenty minutes from Adair. Last night, I made some calls to various theaters in western Illinois, trying to see if I could link Maureen to the area. There are small playhouses peppered throughout that part of the state. A few of them knew a Maura Lewis. Not only does their Maura Lewis match the description of our Maura Lewis, but their version seems to have the same difficulties with certain aspects of the English language. Maureen knew the stories about the woman who had murdered her father. I'm sure she read about Lisa's well-received performance in a play from last year. First, she had to be cast. Maureen Williams was an experienced performer, and she knew exactly what Jenny was looking for—a petulant, childish brat, perhaps one that likes to play peek-a-boo with babies and tell lots of moronic jokes. Once that was accomplished, she developed her plan. Doctor Brown was well-known in the area. He had even been interviewed about his medical efforts in some of the local newspapers."

"How did Maura know that the…"

"Curare."

"How did Maura know the curare would kick in when Lisa was on the balcony?"

"Oh, she didn't. No, no, that was pure happenstance. Maureen had no idea the exact moment Lisa would be paralyzed. She probably had rapturous daydreams about Lisa collapsing at the dining table, seeing everything but not being able to move. Maureen could have whispered rotten nothings in her ear while pretending to be concerned for her." He lit another disgusting cigarette. "Such evil makes the spine shiver. Then, during the party, Maureen followed Allison, didn't she?"

Edward put his head in his hands.

"I'll take that as a *yes*. Now, just for a moment, put yourself in Allison's position. She was alone, in the dark, terrified, with

Maureen waving the straight razor she stole from Allison's bathroom. Allison backed down the wing, trapping herself in the dressing room, the three earrings in her hand. Tell me, what did she do? What would a foolish, desperate girl do in that situation?"

Edward turned white. He whispered, "She swallowed them."

"Ring-a-ding-ding. Why else would the corpse be rummaged through? She must have told Maureen she swallowed them, and the police would find them if Maureen killed her. You and I both know that Maureen is a determined girl. She simply had to *retrieve* them."

Edward shuddered.

"Which brings us to Walter. Maureen was here when I talked with him on the telephone, wasn't she?"

"I'm sorry I lied to you. I knew she was running from something, but I couldn't imagine this."

"Where was she, Edward?"

"Upstairs."

"Listening to our conversation on the telephone?"

He sobbed.

"She went to Adair in a last-ditch attempt to cover her tracks. After Maureen murdered Walter, she discovered the address of Timothy's sister's home in his pocket. 1422 Montrose. Upon returning to Chicago, she found Timothy, overdosed on morphine. She planted the razor and the earrings next to him. It was her best chance to get away with it, a noble effort, considering the corner she had painted herself in." The storm eased. The rain vanished.

Only the dripping gutter could be heard. "The only remaining piece of the puzzle is your Aunt Christine."

Edward's eyes darted upward. "What does she have to do with any of this?"

"We both know Maureen injected her with curare. That's why she went into what the doctors thought was a coma."

"Why would Maura do that?"

"Another superb question. Obviously, she knew you were delivering it to the hospital. She only had to charm her way into your car. Suspicion would naturally be cast on you. Hell, you might even be enough of a jerk to take the blame for her. All Maureen would have to do is stick around and let you pet her, right? As my friend Walter would say, it was like taking candy from the proverbial baby." He snorted a laugh but then quickly composed himself. "Why inject your aunt? It would seem to be an unnecessary attempt at murder. After all, Lisa Pluviam was the target. Why take the risk? I found out the answer in Baraboo."

"What's Baraboo?"

. "It is a town near Devil's Lake. There was a witness who saw the woman accompanying Clarence all those years ago. I traveled to Baraboo with Jenny and Lisa's senior yearbook in the hope that she would be able to identify Clarence's murderer."

"Was she?"

He smiled. "Oh, yes."

"Who murdered him?"

Rowan caught a glimpse of his dull eyes in the mirror. "The

witness pointed at the teacher. The goddamn teacher. I had not noticed the teacher on the page. Christine Filius."

They both felt a tremendous, nervous tension flow through their flesh. Edward ground his teeth.

"It was quite a shock." Rowan chuckled. "I felt like Allison must have felt when she brought Lisa the earrings in the crossover."

Edward's face became pained. He looked away in disgust. "You don't expect me to believe this garbage. Christine?"

"I believe your aunt may have inadvertently revealed it to Maureen."

"But... but how did she inject her?"

"I imagine Maureen had alternate plans in case the earrings did not work—perhaps she carried a syringe with her. I am sure there were plenty at David Brouthers's. We will find out when she is caught. Christine warned us though. She said Maureen tried to kill her."

"Christine gets faces and names mixed up sometimes."

"Maureen killed Lisa Pluviam because she stole her father away from her mother, and she tried to kill Christine because Christine was the one who murdered Clarence Williams."

Edward doddered his head, appearing shell-shocked. "I'm such a fool."

"No, Edward. I am the fool. I knew it was Maura. I always thought so. The signs pointed to her all along."

"What will happen to Christine?"

"I don't know. Her age and health might be considered a factor, but one has to pay for one's crimes. Don't you agree Edward?"

Edward nodded.

"I tell you, out of everything that happened, the biggest shock I received was seeing Maureen's flyer. I knew her name was Williams, but I didn't have proof. Imagine me finding the proof on the wall of my favorite bar. I was even more shocked when I saw her date of birth."

"Why is that?"

"Because Maureen was born in 1919. The girl is only sixteen years old. She couldn't have been Clarence Williams's daughter. That blew my theory of Maureen being the killer out of the water. All of it. Everything I just told you falls apart with that one tiny fact." Rowan chuckled again. "I should have been able to pick up on it. *Hauling ashes* is very popular with teenagers these days. No one over twenty seems to know what it means. My bartender's young nephew knows it though. The phrase is common teenage slang." Rowan shook his head. "Such a shame. I had my heart set on Maureen as the killer. It was a clever theory, don't you think?"

Edward became a still-life portrait, motionless. "You said her name was Williams."

"As my friend Walter told me, Williams is a very popular name. The only name more common in the United States is Washington. She just happened to have the name. Maureen is a runaway teenager from Iowa. Her missing person's flyer has been up in various parts of Chicago for about a month. That's why she wanted nothing to do with the police. The girl would do anything to avoid being captured and returned to her mother. Imagine the spanking she would get. I spoke with her mother before I came here today. The woman is desperate for her little girl to come home. Her husband died in a steel mill accident before Maureen was born. Maureen is all she has left in the world."

Edward suddenly appeared calm, his tense shoulders relaxing back into the sofa and the tears ceasing. For the first time since Rowan's arrival, he smiled.

"I did some theater in high school too, Edward. I was not nearly as good as you. The crying and forgetting the name of the curare again and again—that was good stuff, quite authentic. Everything that comes out of your mouth sounds authentic." Rowan pulled out the twenty-two.

Edward nodded. "Acting is amazing. It teaches you a lot about yourself. You find out what you're really capable of."

Rowan flexed his jaw from side to side until it cracked. "Before Walter was murdered, he sent me a message. Even after death, he was trying to help me. He recommended that I read the playbill. You see, I hadn't paid much attention to the play. My focus was elsewhere. When I read the playbill today, the names of the characters really stuck out. The names are important. Take Allison's character. Her name was Stella. That was the name on the playbill. Stella. Do you remember the balcony scene? Let me see if I can jog your memory. You held up a rose." Rowan held up the gun like a flower, cradling it. *"This is for Agatha.* You said *Agatha*, not Stella. I think Agatha is a special name for you. Agatha Filius was your mother's name. Walter informed me of that as well. I should have made that connection earlier, but I am getting old, Edward. I'm not half the detective I used to be." Rowan's hand shook as it squeezed back onto the handle.

Edward grinned so wide, both rows of teeth showed. "I didn't even mean to do that. It just slipped out."

"Out of all the wrong assumptions I made, two of them proved to be particularly boneheaded. The first was the assumption that Lisa's murder was revenge for Clarence Williams. It was not. Her death was revenge for Agatha Filius. The second was that Christine's poisoning was a murder attempt. Once again I was horribly wrong. Now, before I wipe that fucking smile off your face, let us try a different plot, one that makes absolute perfect sense. Please, tell me if I get anything wrong." He cocked the gun. "Clarence Williams impregnated Agatha Filius. He probably offered to pay for an abortion, but she refused. Clarence left her, and she went mad, eventually dying at the loony bin. Agatha's sister, Christine, murdered him. But you...you Edward were not satisfied. You wanted revenge on the woman who stole Clarence away and drove your mother to madness. You had to kill Lisa Pluviam. Maureen stole the morphine, but you stole the curare. You knew you would be delivering it that day. The post was easy enough, you make deliveries from Glenview, and you know the people that work at the needle plant. You asked Timothy to have the earrings made. He was good friends with the people who work at Eisenberg's. You told him they were to be a present for Maura, and that is exactly what Timothy told them. Of course, you had to test the earrings to make sure the poisoning would work—the whole idea is so outlandish. So you did. You tested them on Christine. You knew you would be at Garfield hospital, and you knew they had an iron lung on the premises that would save her life. To cover up the murder, you butchered Allison Miller. Then you murdered my only friend in the world and parked his body on Main Street in a little town near Iowa. Finally, you went to kill Timothy Brown, but he had already done your work for you. The last step was planting the earrings and the razor next to his dead body. Now that sounds just about right, doesn't it, Ed?"

Edward took a slow, heavy, relaxed breath. *"Oh, drat.* It comes down to luck, Mr. Manory. When it's good, everything falls into place, but when it's bad...*sheesh.* I spent a long time dreaming of killing Lisa. When she came back to Chicago, it was like a gift. It's hard to describe. You see, I'd never left home. Never made anything of my life. I suddenly had a purpose. It was a godsend, really. She was the one I blamed...the one I still blame." He cleared his throat. "My good luck continued when I got cast in the play. I couldn't believe it; I had no experience, but Jenny liked me."

"And the plan?"

"I was down in Glenview when I learned about curare. The plant manager said that in one month, I was going to be delivering something exciting—the next step in modern medicine. That's when it came to me. It's a crazy idea, I mean, you've gotta be a *little* crazy to think of something like that, right? After every rehearsal, Lisa had to wipe blood off her ears and I thought, why not? My hat's off to you. You're right about everything. I knew a guy who worked at the needle plant. I told him I wanted to make needle earrings as an art project, and he pressed two posts for me, even helped me make the little screw housing to put into the glass. He's really nice. Tim knew the jewelers in Eisenberg's. I asked him to make a pair for Maura—identical to Lisa's but using my posts. Testing them on Christine was the scariest thing I've ever done in my life, especially when we ran into that protest. I thought she was done for, but we got to the hospital just in time. Gosh darn commies; they ruin everything. After the test on Christine, I knew it would work. It was the perfect murder. I mean really, it was the *perfect murder*. No one would suspect a thing."

"Not quite. The shipment to the hospital came up short."

"Oh, come on. No one would have checked," Edward frowned with indignation. "Curare is undetectable. How would anyone know what had killed her? And I had a plan for the hospital. I told my supervisor it must have been a mistake, bad paperwork. Of course it was hard for them to buy that excuse when three bottles of morphine were missing too. They must think me a fiend." Edward shook his head. "Oh, Maura."

"Why did you let her go with you to the hospital?"

"Couldn't say no. When women have ignored you all your

life, it feels like true love when one finally pays attention. Besides, she wouldn't know what I'd done. I figured it might be good to have a witness say I didn't do anything. I was even at the reception desk when it happened. No, Maura wasn't a problem. What tripped me up was the hubbub about the note. That gosh darn note. My plan was ruined. I couldn't believe someone else wanted to kill her on the very same night. And the truly horrible thing was, everyone would know that her death wasn't from natural causes. The note said she would be murdered on opening night. I had already switched the earrings and Lisa never left the dressing room—the cop was there and Walter and you…Gee-whiz, talk about bad luck. I should have waited, but I was so excited that I switched them right when I got there in the morning before I learned about the death threat. I had to carry through with it. There was no alternative." Edward giggled. "You know the funny part? When we got past scene two, I thought the curare wasn't working. Christine had gone under a lot quicker. So I dipped Lisa—like when you're dancing. I thought it would make the curare roll into her lobe more. Isn't that amusing? I got a little lucky because she fell off the balcony. At least there was a rational explanation for her death. But I knew you wouldn't accept that. You had to know it was murder. I smashed the one earring, but the bad luck just kept on coming. The other one stayed on. I couldn't get to it. What was even worse was when I checked the drawer for the real earrings, they were gone. I didn't know who had them."

"If Maureen had found the earrings, would you have gutted

her as well?"

Edward bowed his head. "I didn't want to kill Allie. She was so sweet. Poor woman. The plan was to make it look like Timothy committed suicide. I'd slash his wrists with his own razor. I stole it from the bathroom when I went to visit Allie to cheer her up. He was the only one who could tie me to the earrings if anyone figured it out. I had a chance at the party. He was drugged up; I could take him home and he would just go to sleep. It would have been so easy. If the earring trick was ever discovered, well, he was the one who had them made. He was the one with the chemist father. I had to pin it on someone because it wasn't an accident any longer. That's why I was so adamant with you that the writer of the note was the killer. Tim had to die, but…"

"But a more urgent murder came your way."

"That's right. I couldn't believe it when Allie swallowed them. It was disgusting. Well, you saw it. You saw what I had to do."

"Did she beg you for her life?"

"Come now, that's unfair. I'm not proud of it. There was no pleasure in killing her. She didn't suffer—it was less than a minute. I was more worried that Maura had followed her to the theater and seen me leave. I love that girl so much. I'd do anything to protect her. I thought we could have a happy life together, but things just spiraled out of control. I can't really blame her. Pot and kettle, you know."

Rowan blurted, "And Williams?"

Edward shrugged. "It was your fault if you think about it. You put me in a corner. You could have turned this case down. You could have quit after Lisa died and called it an accident. Just couldn't leave it alone though. You—"

The hollow, high-pitched pop of the gunshot rang out through the room. The sound remained in Edward's ears, vibrating with dull echoes, the pungent smell of sawdust and graphite quickly overtaken by that horrifying scent of copper. Edward clasped against the blood spurting from his throat, his body jerking back against the couch.

"That was for Williams." Rowan waited patiently for the last spasm and then turned to the steps.

Upstairs, the old woman was snoring, her lips quivering over raw, pink gums. Rowan pulled a chair to the bed and took out one of Dave Bowen's syringes. He stared at her, trying to see the younger face buried under the old one. "Christine. Christine." He gently patted her arm.

Her eyelids jerked open, but her body remained at ease. "It's you. You're that old detective."

"That's right. I am Rowan Manory."

"Where's Edward?"

"Downstairs. Christine, I want you to tell me all about Devil's Lake. I want you to tell me about Clarence Williams."

She licked her lips. "You know about Clarence?"

"Do you remember what happened?"

"Clarence didn't want to go into the water."

"No?"

"He was scared. He'd almost drowned before. So, I had to convince him."

"How did you manage that?"

"I told him I'd sleep with him, silly. It didn't take much with Clarence. I suggested skinny dipping. A beer and an erection later, he was willing to go in with me. I used to be a decent looking woman if you can believe it. I had beautiful blonde hair. Maybe a little pudgy, but Clarence was never a picky man. I told him I'd keep us tied together with a rope. When we got far enough from land, I untied the knot and swam back just in time to see him go under. I had to do it after what he did to Agatha. I was the one who caught them, him and that little tramp. They were up in the attic. Think about that. He brought her *here*."

"Lisa Pluviam."

"Yes. I heard her voice in the theater. She changed her hair, but I remembered the voice. She was a rotten student, a rotten girl and a terrible actress." Christine stared off to the window. "I think Edward's dating her now. I told him not to do it. She probably wants revenge."

"Your ears are red."

"Edward put those earrings in my ear. I told them they weren't pierced, but he wouldn't listen. Before we left the theater, he shoved them through my lobe. He said it was for a test. It hurt so much." She winced. "Ouch! What was that?"

"Curare. You will remember it soon enough. Tell me, how did you quit smoking? Keep talking to me, Christine. Do not stop."

"I quit a long time ago. My doctor said..." She stopped. Rowan leaned in next to her frozen face. Her chest rose and fell a few more times and then lay still above her dying heart. From her paralyzed tomb, Christine watched the old detective leave the room.

Rowan slumped into Christine's chair and sat motionless, watching the minute hand of the clock move ten times. When he thought the old woman long past the possibility of revival, he went to the telephone.

"Grady, you need to come to the Filius residence straight away. No, two more. The last ones."

17

THE END OF INQUIRY

2:43 p.m. Tuesday, April 17th

A rainbow arced over the eastern part of the city. Sparse drops of rain hid themselves in the air, defiant of the sun's newly restored heat and falling in light-drenched sprinkles. Rowan sat on the top step of the porch. He made a visor with his hands. "Did you catch Maureen?"

Grady paced back and forth over the lawn. His mouth scowled upward, flattening his mustache against his nose. "Young's still looking for the kid."

"The mother informed me she would arrive at Union Station by nine o'clock. It would be nice if Maureen went back with her. We could say that something good came from all this."

Inside the house, the paramedics covered Edward's body with a sheet and discussed how they would go about getting the old woman's body down the stairs.

Grady perched himself on the bottom step, flopping his hat over his knee and squinting at the sun. "At least we won't have to go to that goddamn theater anymore. Getting pretty tired of that place." He slapped at a mosquito on his neck. "I've done dumbass things for a woman, but not quite like you. Not like this…Jesus. I told you not to take the case. I still can't believe you killed an old lady in her nightgown. Just about the most damn cowardly thing I've seen in my fifty-seven years, Manory."

Rowan said, "Williams also told me not to take the case."

Grady's voice lowered to a whispery rasp. "I'm sorry, son. Walter was a good man." He looked off in the distance. "So this crime scene…"

"There is nothing to discuss. I did what I had to, and now you must do the same. You have my confession. I'll sign any paper you put in front of me."

Grady harrumphed. "You, of all people—blowing your wig like that. I know Walter was your friend but…Christ, you killed an old lady. I don't mean to harp on it, but goddamnit!"

Rowan nodded. "You have to take me in Grady. There is no other choice, is there?"

"Yeah well, I worked with your mother. I knew you when you were as tall as my crotch." He was silent for a while. Only the cawing and chirping of birds could be heard. Finally Grady growled and slapped on his hat. "Here's the deal, sport. If there's anything left in that chrome dome, you'll take it. I'll end all inquiries on the opening night murders. Get your affairs in order and then skip town. I don't care where, just not here. And don't tell me your new address neither. I don't want to have to send you a fucking Christmas card every year."

"Awfully benevolent of you, Grady. I was planning on leaving Chicago anyway. Williams always wanted to go to Los Angeles. Perhaps I will make a new identity for myself there." Rowan pushed himself off the steps, staggering onto the walkway.

"Hey, Manory? Did you at least tell Filius that he killed the wrong sister? I mean, before you popped him?"

"I meant to. I had planned it to be the final line. It would have been most satisfying to see the look on Edward's face. But then he said the wrong thing, and my finger...it slipped."

"Pretty good shot. You got him right in the throat."

"I was aiming for his forehead."

Rowan was about halfway down the block when he hailed Young's approaching squad car. Maureen hunkered in the backseat, her hands cuffed in front of her. The sides of her hair draped over her eyes.

Rowan lowered his head to the half-rolled window. "Good afternoon, Maureen. How are we feeling today?"

She brushed her hair aside, revealing black, mascara-smudged tracks of tears running down her face. "Acksherly, I'm not sure. I don't think I'm in the right frame of mind to answer that question. I don't want to go home, Rowan. All my friends are here."

"It is rough, I know."

"Will you tell Eddie what happened? I never meant to hurt him. He must think I'm such a louse."

"I will. Listen, Maureen, I'm sorry I pointed a gun at you. I thought you would have stopped and given yourself up. If I had been a Chicago cop, you'd be in the morgue."

"I was going to pay him back for the morphine. He lost his job because of me."

"That is not important. I have some advice for you. It would behoove you to listen."

"Do you want to hear a joke?" She gave him a plaintive, hopeful look.

Rowan almost gasped. *"A joke?"*

"I thought of it the other day. I haven't told anyone though. I don't know if it's any good. This might be the last chance I have to tell it to somebody who'll get it. My mom doesn't have much of a sense of humor."

The detective's tired shoulders slumped in defeat. "Sure. I'd love to hear it."

"Okay." She propped up her knees on the back seat, leaning close to the window. "How fast was Lisa Pluviam going when she hit the stage?"

"I have no idea."

"Breakneck speed."

He looked at her without expression.

She spoke more slowly. "She was going at breakneck speed."

"I understand."

"Because she broke her neck."

"I get the joke, Maureen. It is...it's funny."

She sniffled. "I can work on the delivery. It probably won't end up in the act."

"Probably, a wise decision. Listen—"

"The set-up would be too long. It'd be too complicated for the audience to follow. Doncha think?"

Rowan's mouth shut. He gave two knocks on the glass, "Well, you take care, Maureen. Be good to your mother. And..." He searched for something to say—something positive he could leave her with. "You were my favorite actor in the play."

Maureen smiled. "You mean...you mean I was better than Lisa?"

"I cannot say *better*. That would be overstatement. You were the most likable. However, in all honesty, that might not be saying much, considering the cast." He bowed and then continued his little shuffle down the sidewalk.

Such a gorgeous day. Why, I can almost hear that awful tune Walter used to whistle. How did it go?

The End

ABOUT THE AUTHOR

This is James Scott Byrnside's second novel. His first, *Goodnight Irene*, was a deliberate attempt to duplicate the thrills and excitement he experienced while reading classic whodunits and impossible crime novels. He has a weakness for locked rooms, footprints in the snow, missing murder weapons, misinterpreted clues, and unreliable suspects. His third novel, a prequel of sorts to both *Goodnight Irene* and *The Opening Night Murders*, will be released in the summer of 2020. It is tentatively titled *The Strange Case of the Barrington Hills Vampire*.

Follow the author on Twitter

MysteryWriter@JamesSByrnside

Or on Facebook

facebook.com/mysterywriting/

Made in the USA
Monee, IL
25 April 2021